FRESH. CURRENT. AND TRUE TO YOU

Dear Reader,

What you're holding is very special. Something fresh, new and true to your unique experience as a young African-American! We are proud to introduce a new fiction imprint—Kimani TRU. You'll find Kimani TRU speaks to the triumphs, problems and concerns of today's black teens with candor, wit and realism. The stories are told from your perspective and in your own voice, and will spotlight young, emerging literary talent.

Kimani TRU will feature stories that are down-to-earth, yet empowering. Feel like an outsider? Afraid you'll never fit in, find your true love or have a boyfriend who accepts you for who you really are? Maybe you feel that your life is a disaster and your future is going nowhere? In Kimani TRU novels, discover the emotional issues that young blacks face every day. In one story, a young man struggles to get out of a neighborhood that holds little promise by attending a historically black college. In another, a young woman's life drastically changes when she goes to live with the father she has never known and his middle-class family in the suburbs.

With Kimani TRU, we are committed to providing a strong and unique voice that will appeal to *all* young readers! Our goal is to touch your heart, mind and soul, and give you a literary voice that reflects your creativity and your world.

Spread the word...Kimani TRU. True to you!

Linda Gill
General Manager
Kimani Press

KIMANI PRESS™

Acknowledgments

God is the source of my talent and blessings.

To my sons who took me back to being a teenager for the sake of this story. To my husband, who is the ringleader of my cheering section. And my family and close friends who keep me grounded.

To my editor, Evette Porter: Thank you for putting *Indigo Summer* on the map and other titles just like it. The minds of our youth depend on the voices in fiction that Kimani TRU books represent.

For my Granny, Rosa A. Heggie:
You are special in so many ways, and the
strongest woman I know. My life is rich because of you.

chapter 1

Indigo

"What kind of name is that for a dog?"

"What, Killer?"

"Yes. That's stupid!"

"What's stupid about it?"

"It just is."

"What kind of name is Indigo?"

"A perfect name, for a perfect girl." I rolled my eyes at him, placed my hands on my hips and was about to give him a piece of my mind. But I decided not to. "How did you know my name anyway?"

He was silent for a moment, standing there with waves all in his hair, as if he slept in a doo-rag or something. His teeth were perfect, and I knew without asking that he used to wear braces. I wished my parents would spring for some braces for me, so that I could have perfect teeth like that. But instead, they were always complaining about having to pay bills and telling me that my teeth weren't that bad.

"Money don't grow on trees, Indi," Daddy was always telling me. "But you got it better than most kids. We provide a nice home for you, you eat good, and you have your own room. That's more than I had when I was your age. I had to share a room with your uncle Keith when I was coming up. Never had my own room." Then he'd go into his spiel about having to walk ten miles to school in a Chicago blizzard. Imagine that. Ten miles in a Chicago blizzard? He'd lose me at that point.

"Daddy, come on," I would laugh. "Ten miles is a lot of miles."

"Don't forget the part about the Chicago blizzard, girl'd have to laugh himself, because he knew that he was only telling half the truth.

Sometimes I loved listening to my daddy's stories about growing up in Chicago at my nana Summer's house. It was an old house, two stories tall, with an old porch and shutters that needed to be painted, but the house always smelled so good. Like fried chicken, or my all-time favorite, macaroni and cheese as only Nana could make. But she was older now, and not quite the Nana I remembered when I was little. She couldn't remember anything anymore, and was always having aches and pains somewhere on her body.

I missed the Nana that would come for visits in the summertime, creep into my room at night with chocolate chip cookies and sit in the wooden rocker next to my bedroom window. I could see my grandmother's caramel face in the moonlight, as she rocked back and forth with her eyes just barely closed.

"Don't get crumbs in the bed, either, little girl," she'd say.

"I won't, Nana." I'd promise, but still have to brush the crumbs from the sheets.

Nana and I would talk about everything we could possibly think of. I could talk to her about any and everything. Whenever something was bothering me, she always knew. Even if I tried to smile and pretend everything was okay, Nana knew. And she'd always make me laugh even when I didn't feel like it.

Nana insisted that I teach her all the latest dances. I taught her how to do the Harlem Shake and had to admit, she had rhythm. Before long, she could do the Harlem Shake better than some of the girls I knew from school.

Nana would come to our house in June and stay the whole summer. I wished she could've stayed the entire year, but she always went back to Chicago at the end of August.

"I gotta go check on my house, baby," she would say whenever I would ask her to stay forever. "But

I'll be back for Christmas. And we'll decorate that old tree together, make hot apple cider and stay up all night on Christmas eve."

"Can I open at least one gift on Christmas Eve?"

"You always do, and end up picking the biggest package under the tree," she'd chuckle. "When will you learn that the best things don't always come in the big packages? Good things come in small packages, too."

She was right, too, because I remembered last year when I got that sapphire necklace with the matching ankle bracelet. It was my favorite gift under the tree, and it came in the smallest package. And in the big box was a bunch of bras, panties and socks—things I didn't care about.

I always cried for a week after Nana was gone.

I'd tell her about all the ugly, stupid boys in my class and tell her how much I hated them.

"You just wait until they grow up," Nana would laugh and say. "You'll like boys one of these days, trust me."

"I don't think so, Nana." I couldn't even imagine looking at a boy for more than ten seconds without being ready to puke. And to like them? Now that was taking it a bit too far. "Why are boys so stupid?"

"I don't know, baby." I could see Nana's smile in

the moonlight; her calmness is what I admired most about her. "They just are. And they don't get much better with age, either. In fact, some of them get worse. You'll see when you get married."

"I'm never getting married, Nana." I wanted to make that crystal clear!

"Never?" Nana would ask with a look of surprise.

"Never!" My mind was made up. She'd see.

And I swore I'd never have kids either. Because if all little kids worked my nerves like my little cousin, Keith Jr. did, then I was never becoming anybody's mama. Good thing I only had to see him on holidays. Since my uncle Keith and his wife were divorced, he only had Keith Jr. every other weekend and on Thanksgiving, during spring break and on the Fourth of July.

It seemed that everybody was getting a divorce, and I hoped that it would never happen to my parents. It happened to my best friend Jade's parents. Just when she thought they were this big happy family, boom, that's when it happened. And it seemed to happen overnight. Her folks had a big argument one night and the next thing Jade knew, her daddy was loading his stuff into the back of a U-Haul. I watched the whole thing from my bedroom window. They lived next door since Jade and I were in the third grade. We had been best friends just that long.

I still remember when they moved in, and Mama

made me go over and introduce myself to the little girl next door. She had baked them a lemon cake and said for me to take it over there. Jade was on her front porch playing with her Barbies, and when she let me see her Barbie doll—and I told her I had four of them at home—it was on. From that day forward we were inseparable.

In fifth grade we had our own Kool-Aid stand, selling beverages to the neighbors as they passed by our little makeshift stand. In seventh grade we both tried out for cheerleading, and neither one of us made the team because we couldn't do the splits. In the eighth grade we played volleyball together, but decided it wasn't our game. We both knew that when we got to high school we'd try out for the dance team. That was our sole purpose for wanting to attend George Washington Carver High, to join their dance team, which was known throughout the city for their outstanding performances. They often performed during parades and stuff, and the whole town recognized their talent. Articles were written about them in the newspaper. To make that team meant you were one of the most talented dancers in all of Atlanta.

It's all we talked about the summer after eighth grade. We spent hours learning all the latest dances and brushing up on our moves. We were determined to make that dance team if it was the last thing we did in this lifetime! But then her folks split up. I never knew that when I watched her daddy load his things into that U-Haul, it was the beginning of the end.

"What your mama cook for dinner?" I remember asking her that day.

"Nothing. She's mad at my daddy."

"What did he do?"

"He came home late again last night," she said, almost in a whisper. "Real late."

"Where do you think he was?"

"I don't know, but she was really mad. They had a bad argument, too," she said. "I don't think they love each other anymore."

"For real?" I asked, lying across my canopy bed and talking to Jade on my cell phone, as she sat on her bed in her room just a spit's distance away.

If I stood in my bedroom window, I could see Jade's pink-and-white comforter on her bed, her bookshelf and the Usher poster she had plastered on her wall. I knew when she brushed her teeth and said her prayers at night, and I knew when she awakened in the morning, because the light from her room would creep across my face and wake me up, too. I would often throw Skittles at her window in order to wake her up when she tried to sleep in on Saturday mornings.

"Yes, for real," she said, almost in tears after her parents' big fight. "She told him to move out."

"Do you think she was serious?"

"He's packing his stuff right now, as we speak," she said.

My heart skipped a beat when she said that. That night, I closed my eyes real tight, knelt beside my bed and prayed that God would not only keep Jade's parents together, but mine, too. I didn't ever want my daddy packing his things and moving away.

I guess he missed the part about Jade's parents, because the next day her father was gone.

Mama had sent me to the new neighbor's with a pound cake. It did something to my heart walking over there, knowing that Jade was gone. Knowing that these new people were living in her house, with different furniture and art of their own on her walls. No longer would I smell her mama's pork chops, smothered in gravy and onions, floating through the air.

"I know your name is Indigo Summer, because I used to sit behind you in Miss Everett's second grade class."

"The boy who used to sit behind me in Miss Everett's class was a bucktoothed ugly boy named Marcus Carter."

"You thought I was bucktoothed and ugly?"

"You're Marcus Carter from the second grade?"

"In the flesh."

I was embarrassed and wanted to crawl under a rock, but I stood there and assessed him from the top of his head, all the way down to his white Air Force Ones. I had to admit, he looked much better than he had in the second grade.

"I still think your dog's name is stupid," I said. "He doesn't even look like a killer."

Marcus held onto the leash which was wrapped tight around Killer's neck.

"You're much prettier than you were in the second grade. I'll give you that," he said.

"What's that supposed to mean?" I rolled my eyes and placed both hands on small hips.

"Well, first of all, you were shaped like a light pole. No shape. Nappy hair. Missing your two front teeth. I see they grew back at least."

"What about you, with your buckteeth and Mister Peabody glasses?" I asked. "It's amazing what braces and a pair of contacts can do, huh?"

"I guess it is. And when do you plan on getting a relaxer on your hair?"

"I don't need a relaxer," I said, and ran my fingers through my wild, thick hair that hung past my shoulders. "I wear my hair naturally for a reason. You don't know anything about hair. Wearing my hair in a natural style represents my heritage, for your information."

"Well, excuse me."

"You're excused," I said and sashayed toward my house, hoping Marcus wasn't watching as I stumbled over the bottom step leading to my porch.

When I turned and saw that he was not only watching, but cracking up, I wanted to choke my daddy for not fixing that step last Saturday.

chapter 2

Marcus

MARCUS Frederick Henry Carter is my name. Marcus, named after Marcus Garvey, a man of color who organized the Universal Negro Improvement Association: an organization designed to bring unity among all blacks and to establish the greatness of the African heritage. Frederick, named after Frederick Douglass who fought to end slavery in America before the Civil War. And Henry. Well, Henry was my great-grandfather's name on my father's side of the family. All I got from my father was his last name, Carter and the wavy hair that every man in our family possessed. My intellect came from my mother. At least that's what she told me.

After my parents divorced two years ago, I ended up living with my pop because Mother relocated back to New Orleans, where her and Pop both grew up.

It was her idea that I live with him. She thought I would receive a better education in the state of Georgia, than I would in Louisiana. And she thought a boy needed his father much more than he needed a mother. I still think she's wrong on that one, because I miss her more and more each day. And I think a boy needs both parents in order to be successful. I still remember when my parents got divorced; it was as if my life stood still. My grades did a nosedive, and I thought I would flunk the eighth grade. It was the therapist my pop took me to who explained that what I was experiencing was depression.

As time went on, things got better. That's when I implemented this master plan of mine: maintaining a four-point-oh grade point average, serving as class president, tutoring kids after school, volunteering in my community…all of this would work to my benefit when I filled out my application for Yale or Princeton, whichever I decided to go to.

Transferring to a different school district was about to mess up my master plan, but trying to explain that to my pop was like pulling teeth. He didn't understand that the high school I was attending in Stone Mountain was a much better school than the new one I'd be attending in College Park. I had done my research, checked out each school and how they panned out on statewide tests. My school could run rings around the ones across town. And the better high school always looked better when trying to apply for college. Not only that, but the better high school would help me to accomplish my master plan. The new school in College Park probably already had somebody groomed for class president, and I wasn't even sure they had a tutoring program. This was all messed up!

I blamed Gloria, my wicked stepmother. She had my pop wrapped around her skinny little finger and jumping through hoops to try and please her. Had him spending some of my college savings on their stupid fairytale wedding; the one where she had too many bridesmaids with ugly dresses. And the tux she made me wear had me sweating like a pig in heat as I had suffered through a photo shoot that seemed to last for hours. And when it was all over, I couldn't see where all my college money had gone.

That's why I definitely had to get a scholarship. Who's to say there would be any money left after Step-Mommy-Dearest was done trying to spend it all.

It was her idea that we move to College Park in the first place.

"Rufus, I need to be close to my mother," she told Pop, as I sat on the steps next to the kitchen eavesdropping on their conversation one morning before school. "She's getting up there in age, and I need to be able to take her to her doctor's appointments and to the grocery store. It takes forever just to get over there to her from where we live now. And God forbid she has an emergency."

She's a drama queen, I thought, as I laced up my Air Force Ones.

"Why don't we just move Evelyn over to this side of town?" Pop tried to reason with her. "I've got a nice little piece of property just two blocks from here. It wouldn't take much work to fix it up for your mother."

That's what my pop did for living. Fixed up old houses and rented them out. Or sold them, whichever made him the most money. Since before I was born, he and my grandfather owned the same real estate investment company; the family business is what they called it. After Granddad passed away, my father inherited the family business, and talked of passing it on to me. Every chance he got, he was pressuring me about working with him, wanting to teach me the odds and ends of the business. He couldn't wait for my graduation day, so I could start full-time the day after.

The problem was, I wasn't interested in selling or managing real estate. And the family business was definitely not my idea of a future. I had my master plan and I was going to college. I wanted to do something more meaningful with my life than manage a bunch of run-down properties. That's where Pop and I bumped heads. We each had a different plan for my future.

Killer, my German Shepherd, plopped his huge body down next to me on the step, licking on my shoe, and trying to chew on my shoestrings until I smacked him.

"Stop, dude!" I said and made a mental note to give his stinking behind a bath when I got home from school that day. I didn't want Gloria fussing about the dog smell in the house again. My backpack at my feet, I removed my doo-rag and brushed my waves as I continued to listen to the Drama Queen plead her case to my father.

"Rufus, you know Mama. She ain't gonna move to Stone Mountain and leave her house. Not the house that her and Daddy shared all those years," Gloria said. "And all her friends are right there in the neighborhood where she lives."

"I understand, Gloria."

That was all Pop said that day. But next thing I knew, a RE/MAX sign was stuck in the middle of our front yard. Our house sold a lot faster than Pop and Gloria had expected and the new owners were anxious to move in and wanted us out. Before I knew it, we were packing our stuff into boxes. The problem was, we had nowhere to go. She and Pop had looked at dozens of houses in the newer subdivisions of College Park, but Gloria couldn't seem to settle on one that she liked. She had to have the perfect house, with custom-made cabinets, the master bedroom had to be a certain square footage, and it needed to have a certain number of windows. She actually would walk through each house counting windows. Wow!

"Why don't we just have a house built?" She finally made a suggestion.

"But where do we go while our house is being built?" Pop asked.

"We can move into one of your rental properties temporarily."

"That would be fine, Gloria, but the problem is, I don't have any available on that side of town."

"Don't you have any tenants who are behind on their rent?" I could just picture that wicked little smile of hers. "One who's just begging to be evicted?"

"They're all a little slow paying, Gloria, but I work with them. Always have. They're good working-class people who just fall behind from time to time. That's all."

"What about that woman in the property on Madison Place? The one whose husband left her. You've given her more than enough time to get caught up. And now that her husband is gone, she struggles just to make the rent every month. It's always late, and sometimes short," she said. "That's a cute little house too, and I love it so much, Rufus!"

"That family has lived in that property for nearly fifteen years," Pop said. "I wouldn't feel right asking Barbara to leave. And she's got those children...and..."

"I thought you wanted me to be happy." I would've bet my lunch money that Gloria's lip was all poked out as she began pouting, and I could just see her rubbing her index finger across my father's face. "You could put her in one of your smaller places. You could put her in that place just two blocks from here."

Pop's demeanor softened. I could tell. He was falling under her spell.

"I *could* talk to Barbara. See if she wants that old place. It's a lot older than the one she lives in now, but I could fix it up for her," Pop reasoned. "The rent over here would be a little cheaper than what she's paying now. That way she wouldn't be out on a limb every month. She'd have to uproot her kids and send them to another school, but..."

"It's better than being homeless," Gloria added.

"If I'm going to do it, I'd better do it before school starts again in the fall."

"Is that a yes?" Gloria asked my father.

"I'll call Barbara when I get to the office," he said.

Gloria always seemed to get her way no matter what.

* * *

On moving day, I carefully placed all my CDs—50 Cent, T.I., Kanye West—into a cardboard box. Packed away my DVDs—*Friday, Next Friday, Friday After Next*, and some of my old Kung Fu movies—into the same box. And I couldn't forget my all-time favorite DVD, *Rush Hour,* and every episode of *The Dave Chappelle Show,* which was packed in the same box. I didn't want the movers packing my sacred items. I needed to pack them myself, to make sure they made it to the new place safely.

I placed the box on the backseat of my '92 Jeep Cherokee that I'd saved up for and bought with money that I had earned by working the drive-thru at Wendy's. As 50 Cent's "Just A Little Bit" blasted through my speakers, Killer took his place in the passenger's seat of my Jeep, his head hanging out the window as I pulled out of the subdivision I grew up in…a place where I had chased the ice cream man down the street at full speed every day just to buy a red, white and blue bomb pop; the same neighborhood where I had my first kiss with Ashley Thomas right in between Mrs. Fisher's house and the vacant house at the end of the block, the place where I was chased by Mr. Palmer's Doberman every time I took the short cut through his yard, and where I fell out of the tree in Miss Booker's front yard and broke my arm when I was nine; the same place where I pushed a lawn mower up and down the street and made money cutting lawns every summer since I was twelve, and where the entire neighborhood gathered for cookouts and block parties every Memorial Day, Fourth of July, and on Labor Day.

The neighborhood was all a kid like me had. That and Kim Porter, the girl who broke up with me the same day she found out that I was moving to the south side.

"It's too hard trying to go out with somebody at another school, Marcus," she'd said.

Then she said those four words that pierced my heart.

"Let's just be friends."

The words still rang in my head, long after they had lingered in the air. *Let's just be friends.*

My life as I knew it was over.

chapter 3

Indigo

MY breasts had grown a little bit over the summer, even though I was still in the same A-sized cup, I could tell they were just a little bit bigger than they were at the beginning of the summer. I wore my pink low-cut top that I'd picked up at the mall on Saturday just to show them off a little, my low-cut Mudd jeans and pink, black and white FILAs.

The first day of school was not the same without Jade. We'd made so many plans before she moved away. Times had gotten too hard for her mother and she decided that they should move in with Jade's grandmother in New Jersey. Jade hated living there, too, because her grandmother was nothing like Nana. She was mean and stuffy, Jade told me, and she made them go to church three nights a week and on Sunday, too. She hoped it wouldn't be long before her mama found them an apartment or something. She'd have to find a job first, and that was the hard part. Thank God for free nights and weekends, because I was able to call Jade every night after nine o'clock from my cell phone. And we talked all day on Saturdays and Sundays. That helped, although it still wasn't the same as having her next door.

On the first day of school, I was forced to walk to the bus stop with Angie Cummings, who was literally "a nobody" on the face of the earth. She was a smart kid who made straight As and wore what looked like her Grandma Esther's clothes to school. I was more of a B student, and sometimes C when I didn't apply myself as much. I wanted to make good grades, but sometimes I just got caught up in other stuff and didn't pay as much attention in class. For people like Angie, who didn't have a life, straight As came much easier for them.

Even though I'd known Angie since kindergarten, and we attended the same church, she wasn't someone I hung out with. She was kind of weird and wore bifocals. But since she was going to the bus stop, and I was going at the same time, there was no harm in walking together, although she was the type of person that would ruin your reputation for life. And I'd worked too hard for my popularity. Outside of the cheerleaders, Jade and I were the most popular two girls at our middle school because we could dance so well.

It was hard being popular, too, because people were always trying to be friends with me. And boys were always trying to talk to me, telling me how cute I am, and making comments about my body. Now that's what really got on my nerves, the comments about my body. My body was the one thing that made me uncomfortable, because it was always changing. I knew how smart I was, knew I could dance, and I could beat everybody, even Nana, in a game of Monopoly. But when it came to my body, now that was a whole different story. My breasts were always changing, and I wasn't built like a light pole anymore. There were bumps growing in some places, lumps in others, and my hips were filling out a little. Even my booty was coming full circle, and was more round than I remembered it being in the fifth grade. Now that was weird, but the weirdest thing of all came three years ago, sixth grade, right after recess was over one day on the playground. I remember it just like it happened yesterday.

Miss Brown had blown her whistle to let us know that it was time to come inside. It was after lunch, and it was on a Friday. I remember because I was so excited that Nana Summer was coming for a visit that weekend, and I knew she'd be at my house by the time I got home from school. My stomach had been cramping for about three days, and when I told my mother about it, she gave me some Midol and asked, "You started your period, Indi?"

"No, ma'am."

"Well, if you're having cramps, it probably means that it's coming soon."

"What's it for, Mama?" I asked her, "I mean, why do women have periods?"

"All women do, Indi. It's just a part of life." That was all my mother said, before she took me to the CVS drugstore and bought me sanitary products and told me how to use them. I could tell that she was just as uncomfortable talking about it as I was.

So I left it alone, until that day on the playground when I felt a warm gush in my underpants and I took off running at full speed to the restroom. It was the most embarrassing moment of my life, and on the bus all the way home, my jean jacket tied around my waist, I felt like a freak or something. Thought all of my classmates were staring at me. As if they'd all known.

I was so happy to see Nana standing in our kitchen when I got home. I grabbed her around the waist, and hugged her so tightly from behind.

"Can we talk?" I whispered in her ear, as she stirred something on the stove. It smelled like spaghetti. "In my room?"

"Sure, baby," she said, turned the fire down underneath the pot and followed me to my bedroom. "What is it?"

"Do I look different today?"

"Different how?" she asked.

"Do I look more grown-up than I did the last time you saw me."

"A little taller maybe. But I was just here at Christmastime, Indi. What's this about?"

"It came today," I whispered. I didn't want the rest of the world hearing, and certainly not my daddy if he was anywhere in the house. Surely she knew, just as everyone else probably did. Even Jade had seemed standoffish that day.

"What came today?" Nana asked.

"You know," I said. "I started it."

"Indi, what on earth are you talking about?" Nana asked, feeling my forehead with her back hand. "Are you feeling okay, you look a little flush."

"I got my period today, Nana," I whispered.

"Oh, that's what this is all about." She laughed a little, as if this was funny. How could she laugh, when my insides were in turmoil? "Perfectly natural thing for a girl your age, Indi. We've all traveled this road before."

"What's it all mean, Nana?"

"Well, it means that you're not a little girl anymore.

You're a young lady now. And you have to conduct yourself as such."

"It means I can't play with my Barbies anymore?" I asked, already torn by the decision to continue to play with them or to pack them away in a cardboard box. Twelve was such an awkward age. You don't know whether to play or act grown-up.

"You can play with your Barbies as long as you want," she said. "But you should also start thinking about other things, like helping your mama out around this house, cleaning up behind yourself a little more, making better grades in school. You need to be more responsible."

"Why do we have to have menstrual cycles, Nana? Does it have something to do with boys?"

"Well, it means that now you can become pregnant," Nana said, taking a seat on the edge of my bed and inviting me to sit down next to her. "Every month your body produces an egg which travels through what's called your fallopian tubes, and on down to your uterus." Nana drew a line with her fingertips to show me where my fallopian tubes began and where my uterus began. "In order to prepare for this egg, your uterus creates this thick lining to make a nice cushion for it."

"What's the egg for?" I frowned.

"The egg comes to connect with the sperm of a

man in order to make a baby." Nana wiped sweat from her forehead with the back of her hand. "That's why it's even more important now that you don't fool around with boys."

"I hate boys anyway."

"You won't always hate boys. In fact, you'll grow to like them very much. And you'll find yourself in situations where your hormones will get the best of you."

"What are hormones?"

"That's a whole other discussion. We'll talk about that another time," Nana said. "Now as I was saying, the purpose of the egg coming is to connect with the sperm. But the two should never connect until you're married to the man of your dreams and you have both talked about starting a family. You understand?"

"Yes."

"And until that time, every month, your body will still produce that old egg, and in anticipation for it, your uterus—" she drew a line with her fingertips again "—will always make this nice cushion for it. Think of it as a pincushion, like the one I use when I'm hemming your dresses."

"A pincushion?" I almost fell out laughing.

"Yes, a pincushion." Nana smiled. "And after a little while, when the uterus sees that it no longer needs the extra blood and tissue, that old pincushion will begin to dissolve itself."

"And that's when my period comes?"

"That's right," she said. "Every month like clock-work. At least until you get to be my age."

"Your body doesn't make pincushions anymore, Nana?"

"It's a whole lotta things my body don't do any-more." She laughed. "You just keep on living, child. You'll see."

"I love you, Nana."

"I love you, too, baby." She took my breath away when she hugged me. "Now come on in here and help me with dinner. But first I want you to get this room cleaned. And do it without your mama having to ask you to sometimes. Okay?"

"Okay, Nana."

That day my Barbies had been packed into a card-board box, never to surface again.

"I heard Jade moved to New Jersey," Angie said as we made our way to the bus stop.

"Yep." I tried to keep the conversation at a minimum just in case someone was watching.

"You talked to her?"

"Every day."

"Does she like it there?"

"No. She hates it," I said. "Never wanted to move there in the first place."

"I know," Angie said. "It's a shame how they got put out like that."

"Put out?" I asked. "They didn't get put out."

"Well, my mom works with the owner of the property's wife, and I heard my mom talking to someone on the phone who said that Jade's mama didn't pay her rent on time and they got evicted."

"Well, that person your mom was talking to on the phone didn't know what she was talking about," I said. "Jade's mama wanted to move to New Jersey."

"That's not what I heard."

"Well, you should get your facts straight before you go spreading rumors."

"Okay," Angie said, not wanting to get into confrontation. "You going to the Homecoming Dance?" she asked, changing the subject.

"I don't know. If somebody asks me, I might."

"That's nice. I'll probably be at home studying." She snickered, as we approached the others at the bus stop.

Angie just sort of vanished into a nonexistent state, and Bo Peterson started working on my nerves the minute I laid eyes on him.

"Well, well, well. If it isn't Indigo Summer," he said. "Where's your sidekick?"

"Why are you talking to me, Bo?"

"Gonna be kinda lonely for you without Jade

around," he said. "Got you hanging out with the likes of Angie Cummings. Angie your new best friend?"

"We're not hanging out," I said, my eyes glancing over at Angie, and then looking away. I wasn't trying to hurt her feelings. "Shut up, Bo!"

"You gon' start dressing like her Grandma Esther, too?" he asked.

All of his boys started laughing, and I just rolled my eyes. This was exactly why I told Nana that boys were stupid.

I glanced back down the block, at the house next door to mine. I don't know why, but I wondered where Marcus was—if he'd overslept. I wondered if he would be riding the bus, or if he got dropped at school. Suddenly, he appeared on his front porch wearing baggy black jeans and a white tee, a backpack thrown across his shoulder. Excitement rushed through me as I waited for him to step off the porch and head toward the bus stop. Instead, he stepped off of his porch and headed toward the old white Jeep that was parked in front of his house. He hopped into the driver's seat and started it up. Pulled off. A sophomore with his own car. Imagine that.

Guess my idea of offering him the seat next to me on the bus was not an option.

chapter 4

Indigo

The hallway was crowded as I pushed my way through hordes of students gathered at lockers, talking, laughing and catching up on old times. Several students just sort of wandered through the hallway, most of which were freshmen—and lost, like me. I took another glance at my schedule and tried my best to find Room 17A, Miss Petersburg's home room class. But the numbers seemed to be getting larger, as I made it to the end of the hall and stood in front of Room 25C.

"You lost?"

Standing before me was the most beautiful pair of brown eyes that I'd seen in all of my fifteen years.

"Looking for 17A," I told him.

"Oh, you got Miss Petersburg for home room." The beautiful creature was dressed in an orange-and-black football jersey—the school's colors—number

84 plastered across the front. He took my schedule from my hand, gave it a look over. "You're on the wrong floor, girl. Room 17A is on the first floor."

"Oh."

"You a freshman, huh?" he asked.

"Yes."

"I'm Quincy," he said, "you want me to walk you to your class or what?"

If I could've stopped my heart from beating so fast, I would've answered his question. But when I opened my mouth to say something, nothing leapt out.

He just started walking beside me, as the bell shook the walls in the hallway.

"Is that the tardy bell?" I asked, not wanting to be late on my first day.

"Naw, it was just the warning bell," he explained. "It means you got three minutes to get to class. But they give you extra time to find your classes on the first day of school."

"Oh."

"What's your name?"

"Indigo," I managed to say. "Indigo Summer."

"That's a different name," he said. At least he didn't say it was stupid. "Were you named after somebody?"

"No."

"That's a weird name." His smile seemed to give light to the entire school. "But it's cute, though."

"Thank you," I said, hoping that was the proper response, and that I didn't sound too stupid.

"You going to homecoming?"

Everyone seemed to be asking that question.

"When is it?" I asked. There were so many activities going on the first few weeks of school, I was just overwhelmed by all of it.

"The game is Friday night. I'll be starting. Linebacker." He smiled, obviously proud of his position on the football team. "The dance is on Saturday."

We stopped in front of my classroom. He handed my schedule back to me.

"Here we are. This is 17A," he said. "You wanna go with me on Saturday night or what?"

"Well, I...I hadn't...um..." I wasn't prepared for a question like that. "Okay."

"Cool," he said. "I'll meet you here after class and you can give me your phone number. You do have a phone, don't you?"

"Yeah."

"Cool. I'll see you later then."

I watched as Quincy trotted down the hallway, his jeans sagging just a little in the back, bold black letters on the back of his orange jersey, RAWLINS...84.

He vanished, but the smell of his Michael Jordan cologne lingered.

* * *

The sign on the wall outside the gym read: DANCE TEAM TRYOUTS TODAY, 4:00 PM.

So many girls on the bleachers, chattering about which classes were hard, and which ones you could get an easy A in, which boys were cute, and which ones looked like toads, and which teachers got on their ever-lovin' nerves. At my old middle school, I knew just about everybody, but at this new school, as I looked around the huge gymnasium, I realized I was just another face in the crowd, and I didn't know anyone. And my confidence about making the dance team was now shaken after seeing some of these girls, with much rounder hips, and much better moves, shake what their mamas gave them. Some of them were really good, making my routine, the one that Jade and I had worked on for months, seem just ordinary.

I took a seat on the bleachers, as a woman blew a whistle to get our attention. The chatter ceased.

"Ladies, let's get started," she said. "I'm Miss Martin, and I'm over the dance team here at George Washington Carver. Keisha here will be assisting me today with the music. If you're trying out, you should have your own CD or tape with your music on it. Make sure that it's the edited version of whatever song it is. This is the first round. Fifteen of you will be lucky enough to come back tomorrow for round two."

"How will we know who made it to round two?" A dark, round girl at the other end of the bleachers asked.

"Tomorrow morning, a list of those who made the cut will be posted outside the cafeteria," she said. "Good luck to you all. Now, let's get started. First on my list are Tameka Brown and Michelle Smith."

Tameka and Michelle both stepped down from the bleachers, Tameka handed Keisha a CD, told her which track to play, and stood in the middle of the shiny floor waiting for the music to begin.

My heart pounded as Nelly's "Shake Ya Tail-feather" echoed through the gym, and their bodies began to gyrate to the sound of it. Wearing matching black T-shirts and black shorts, their moves were calculated as they bounced to a rhythm similar to each other's. Nothing original, just a mixture of the Harlem Shake, the Tick and another dance that I didn't recognize. I sat there with my chin resting in my hands, my insides in turmoil for the entire four minutes and nine seconds that their song lasted, awaiting my turn. When it was over, they took their seats on the bleachers.

Miss Martin wrote some notes on the pages attached to her clipboard.

"Indigo Summer." She said my name in her own southern version of it. I hadn't expected my turn to come so soon. "You're up next."

As I leaped from the bleachers, my pink, black and white FILAs hitting the shiny wooden hardwood floor, I handed Keisha Thomas my CD to put in.

"Track three," I told her, as music from Usher's new CD took me to a world of my own. A place where Jade was, with laughter and the hard work that we'd put into our routine, spending hours studying Usher's video, and trying to emulate his moves. And we had them down to an art. Usher, our artist of choice. Well, Jade's artist of choice. She thought he was the most beautiful person who ever walked the face of the earth, with his smooth chocolate skin and kissable-looking lips, as she put it. She had every CD he ever made and dreamed of bumping into him at Publix grocery store or Wal-Mart someday.

"You know he lives in Atlanta, right?" She reminded me of that fact every chance she got.

"I doubt that you'll see him at Publix or Wal-Mart, Jade."

"He gotta buy groceries, girl."

"I'm sure he has someone who shops for him," I said. "And I doubt if he shops at Wal-Mart anyway."

"Well if I ever see him, I'm rushing him. Just want you to know that."

"And I'll act like I don't know you."

"I hope I don't say anything stupid."

"You will," I assured her.

Then her eyes would get all glossy, like she was fantasizing about him or something.

"Yep, I probably will."

We'd spent hours working on our routine, a routine made for two people, but here I was forced to perform it alone.

"You can do it," Jade had told me on the phone the night before. "You don't need me there. You know the moves better than me."

I prayed she was right as the music resonated through my body, and I mimicked Usher's moves that we'd practiced for months. I was a little stiff at first, but as the music came to life inside of me, I loosened up a little. I pretended I was on Jade's front porch again, in control, the bass from the music shaking the wooden boards. And the girls who stared at me from the bleachers were faceless and nameless fans, wishing they were me. Wishing they could move like me. I was lost in the rhythm.

As Usher sang, "I'm so caught up…" my legs took on a life of their own. Thought about the video that we'd played over and over again. I took a bow as the last few lyrics resonated through the gym.

"Thank you, Miss Summer." Miss Martin's southern twang brought me back to the present time. She jotted down a few notes on her clipboard. I took my CD from Keisha and plopped down on the bleachers, sweat resting on my top lip.

"You were good," Tameka whispered.

"Thanks. So were you," I whispered back.

"Hope I was good enough to make the team," she said.

"Hope I was, too."

I used the sleeve of my shirt to wipe sweat from my face.

chapter 5

Marcus

COACH Robinson's whistle sounded across the field.

"Let's run that play one more time," he said, his voice loud for a man his size. Coach Robinson was about five-foot-seven, dark, a short dude with a receding hairline. He was buff though, obviously from pumping iron each day.

I wasn't much of a football player anymore, had played when I was little, but never really had a desire to play sports. I was too busy studying and volunteering my time to worthy causes, and tutoring people who sucked in math.

But Coach Robinson, who was my American History teacher at this new school in College Park, had immediately taken a liking to me. He called on me more times on the first day of school than anyone else in the class; to answer questions and to help pass out worksheets. When the bell sounded for me to head to my next class, he called my name.

"Mr. Carter." He looked up from his desk, and motioned for me to come back.

I walked slowly back to his desk. "Yes, sir?"

"How come you're not on my football team?"

"I don't really have time for sports, Coach. Got a lot on my plate with my schoolwork," I explained. "Plus I'm working toward getting a scholarship, and I wanna get it based on my grades, not my ability to run a football down the field. I got a part-time job, too."

I was able to transfer to a different Wendy's on the other side of town. I was grateful for that, because I definitely needed my own money.

"You're Rufus Carter's boy, aren't you?" he said.

My pop was a pillar in the community; people from miles around knew him and respected him. For years, he and my grandfather had sponsored sports teams, donating money for equipment and uniforms. The name of his company, Carter's Affordable Homes, was plastered on the back of T-shirts and on plaques all over town.

"I remember when you played for the community center over there in Stone Mountain. You were pretty doggone good," he said. "I used to coach at the community center here in College Park. I remember you."

"I played quarterback."

"And you were good, too," he said. "You took that team to victory every single year. Why don't you play anymore?"

"Lost interest."

"You sure you don't wanna give this team a try?" he asked. "Quincy Rawlins is my starting linebacker, but I'd like to try you as a wide receiver or cornerback."

"I don't know. It's been a while since I played."

"Well if you change your mind, you always got a spot on the team."

"Thanks, Coach." I folded the worksheet which was my homework assignment and placed it inside my book. "I'll keep that in mind."

Curiosity had brought me there, as I sat on the bleachers on the football field and watched them practice. My mind went back to the days when football was my first love; my everything and then some. Nothing was more important to me back then. But it had soon become a long forgotten dream, and I remember the person who had shattered it: Mr. Forbes.

I worked my behind off that year to make the team, had pumped weights all summer just trying to build up my muscle mass, had gone to football camp and everything, but the coach at my middle school didn't think I had what it took to play quarterback anymore.

"It's a new day, Carter," Mr. Forbes, the new blond-haired, pale-faced coach, had gripped his clipboard, said and frowned. "The days of you getting what you want because your daddy owns half of this town is over."

"But Coach, I played quarterback for the community center for five years straight."

"Well this is not the community center, and I've got a quarterback." He smiled. "His name is Todd Richmond."

"Todd ain't half as good as me."

"Ain't?" He repeated my bad English. "Ain't is not the proper word to use in that sentence. I swear to God I don't know why I took this teaching job over here. Should've stayed in the suburbs where the students are both smart and talented. Over here, you people think that just because you can run a football down the field, that you don't have to know anything else. You go through school with blinders on, thinking that sports will save you from your ignorance."

I stood there eyeballing him, my blood boiling as he pretty much called me and my entire race stupid to my face. I knew I had to prove him wrong. Knew that I had to prove that not every black kid who was good in sports was dumb in the classroom.

"My grades are good," I said in my defense.

"You're in the low Cs, kid. I'm struggling just to keep you on the team."

"But I'm bringing them up," I said. "They dropped

when my parents got divorced, because I was stressing over that."

"It's always an excuse with you youngsters," he said.

"It's true," I told him. "I'm going to bring them back up. And when I graduate, I'm graduating with honors."

"You see Todd over there?" He pointed toward the redhead who'd stolen my position on the team. "When he leaves high school, he'll not only have had four good years of football, but with his grade point average, he's sure to get a scholarship to Yale or Princeton. And that's a fact."

"I could get a scholarship to Yale or Princeton if I wanted to."

"Not likely," he said, as if it was the most ridiculous thing he'd ever heard. "But there's no doubt you could get into either Morehouse or Clark-Atlanta University, one of the historically black colleges here in Atlanta. That is, if you bring that grade point average up, and keep it steady during your high school years. But you have to really be a special kid to get into an Ivy League school like Yale or Princeton, Marcus."

His words stuck with me, tore me up inside, and even stopped me from sleeping a few nights. I knew what I had to do. I had to come up with a Master Plan. I wanted to go to Yale or Princeton, simply to set a standard; to prove a point. Not that Morehouse or Clark-Atlanta weren't good schools, because they were. In fact, Morehouse was known for its strong math and science programs. And I was a math scholar, could work problems out with my eyes closed. But I wanted to not only get accepted to a school where statistically blacks weren't accepted, but I wanted to get a scholarship to one, too.

Football was over for me that day, and I was determined to make straight As, graduate with honors, get a scholarship to Yale or Princeton and look for that Mr. Forbes one day and show him that he was wrong about Marcus Carter. I dreamed of that day.

Coach Robinson had the team running a play over and over again, and when he was sure it was burned into their memory, he ran it again. I pulled my worksheet out of my American History book, looked over the questions. They were simple, so I completed it, the sun beaming down on my fresh haircut as I sat in the bleachers. I scribbled my name across the top, then folded the worksheet back up, stuck it into my book and placed my book into my backpack. Threw my backpack across my shoulder and decided to head over to the gym where the girls were trying out for the dance team. Nothing like watching a bunch of girls shaking it up.

I pulled the heavy door open, peeked inside, Usher's

"Confession," ringing in my ears as I stepped inside. Took a seat on the bleachers next to some other guys who'd stayed after school just to watch the girls move their hips to hip-hop music. They were picking out which ones they would ask out, and saying how cute Indigo Summer was as she bounced to the music that echoed throughout the gymnasium. Just by looking at her, I couldn't tell that she could move like that. But she could. She was good, and I was glad that I had caught the end of her performance.

After the last group of three girls started dancing to some song by Ludacris, I decided to make my way outside the gym, and stand near the glass doors. I didn't want to miss Indigo when she came out. I wanted to speak to her; maybe offer her a ride home. Tell her how good her performance was. My backpack thrown across my shoulder, as girls passed by whispering, smiling and waving, I waited patiently.

"Hey," one of them said. "You Marcus Carter?"

"Yep," I said.

"You're in my fourth period." The light brown girl smiled a cute little smile, and my eyes found her cleavage that she was showing too much of.

"Oh," is all I could say as I thought back to all the girls in my fourth period. I didn't remember her face.

"I sit two seats behind you in class," she said. "I'm Alicia."

"Nice to meet you."

"And I'm Shauna," her friend said. "You going to the homecoming dance?"

"I don't know. I hadn't really thought about it."

I wondered if Indigo was going, and if so, if she already had a date. Maybe I'd ask her.

"Well, if you decide to go, who you taking?" Alicia asked.

"I don't know."

"Well, I don't have a date," she smiled.

My eyes found the door of the gym as they swung open and the girls trying out for the dance team rushed out. I searched for Indigo in the crowd, and spotted her walking and talking with another girl. She wore pink shorts and a white top that hugged her small breasts. Her wild hair fell softly onto her shoulders, and her skin was flawless.

"Indigo," I called her, walking away from Alicia and Shauna, leaving their questions and comments to dissolve into the air.

Indigo's eyes found mine.

"What's up?" She asked.

"I been waiting on you. Wanted to tell you how good you were in there."

"Thanks. Hope I make the team," she said dryly, as if she doubted her own skills.

"You will," I said.

"What you doing hanging around in the girls' gym anyway?" she asked.

"Watching the tryouts."

"You stayed after school just to watch us dance? Don't you have anything better to do?" she asked, frowning. "Why aren't you on the football team or something?"

"Because I don't play football...anymore," I said. "But I watched the team practice for a while. Then I decided to come over here and see what was up with the dance team tryouts."

"Well, good for you," she said and walked away from me, through the glass doors and to the outside courtyard.

I followed.

"You got a ride home?"

"My father's picking me up," she said, searching the lineup of cars that sat at the curb; parents waiting for their children to come out.

"...'cause I was gonna say, I could give you a ride, since you live right next door."

"That's alright. He's already here," she said, and took off toward her father's truck.

Didn't say goodbye. Just left me standing there, unaware that I thought she was the finest girl in the entire school.

chapter 6

Indigo

Pushing my way through the crowd, I made it up to where the list was plastered on the wall. My heart pounding, my mind drifting back to Miss Martin's words, "...tomorrow morning, a list of those who made the cut will be posted outside the cafeteria." Who would've thought that a list, a piece of paper taped to the wall, which held the names of fifteen girls who made the first round of dance team tryouts, would cause so much chaos? The fifteen girls whose names appeared on that list had been handpicked by Miss Martin, who had been the dance team coach for at least ten years. She had delivered an impeccable dance team year after year, one that was considered to be the best in the metro Atlanta area. Making that list meant that she thought you were good enough to come back for a second look; good enough to potentially carry on the school's legacy. Meant that she thought you were better than the fifteen other girls whose names did not appear on the list.

As I reached the list, my French-manicured nail scanned the names until I got about three quarters of the way down the page. There it was in bold black letters against white paper, INDIGO SUMMER. The sight of it made me want to dance through the hallway; made me want to jump and shout. Made me want to pull out my cell phone and call Jade right at the moment and tell her the good news, but I knew better than to use my parents' daytime minutes for anything other than emergencies. I did that before and ended up getting my phone repossessed for a month. It's hard being cut off from the rest of the world like that. My cell phone was my lifeline. To cut that off would be like cutting off my air circulation.

I had made the first cut! I closed my eyes for a brief moment and thanked God. He'd obviously heard my prayer the night before and that morning on the bus. He was probably tired of me bugging him. But bugging him paid off, because he came through for me. Again.

The second name from the top of the list was Tameka Brown's. She'd made the first cut, too. The problem was, her dance partner Michelle Smith's name was not on the list.

Michelle's eyes were bloodshot as she leaned up against the wall.

"I don't see how she picked you and not me," Michelle was saying to Tameka. "We were a team. Did the same moves and everything. I don't know what happened."

"I don't know either," Tameka told her, looking for words that would console her friend, but she was at a loss for them.

"It's not even fair. I can't stand Miss Martin!" Michelle said and then stormed on down the hall.

Tameka shrugged as she spotted me.

"Congratulations," I said.

"Same to you," she said. "I knew you would make it."

I'm glad she was so sure, because I hadn't been. I'd tossed and turned the entire night before thinking about it. By the time I had finally drifted off, it was almost time to get up, get showered and dressed for school.

I was more than surprised to see my name on that list. My heart pounded as I thought about the second round. Round two might not be so generous.

"Heard you made the first cut for the dance team." Quincy found me at my locker, pulling my world geography book out for my next class. Dressed in blue jeans and a Michael Vick jersey, he smelled so good. News sure did travel fast.

"Yeah, the second round is after school today," I said, slamming my locker shut and pulling my book to my chest. My heart started to flutter and the palms of my hands got all moist at the sight of him.

"I didn't even know you could dance," he said with those kissable-looking lips. Jade should see these lips. She would compare them to Usher's. I found myself wondering what it would be like to kiss them, especially since I hadn't kissed a boy since I kissed Andre in the seventh grade. And his lips weren't nearly this kissable looking. "If I didn't have football practice I would come and check you out."

I thanked God that football practice and dance team tryouts took place at the same time. His being there would make me nervous and I would probably mess up my entire routine. I was grateful.

"Yeah, it's too bad you got practice."

Before I knew it, his lips were against mine, and for at least ten seconds I stopped breathing. I closed my eyes, wanting to savor the moment that Quincy Rawlins kissed Indigo Summer for the first time. I could've sworn I saw sparks flying after I opened my eyes. His eyes were opened the whole time, watching me.

"Well, I gotta get to class. I'll check you later," he said, walking backwards and then disappearing into a crowd of students.

I wondered if he had felt the same butterflies in his stomach.

The gymnasium was packed with people wanting to see who would make the second round of the dance team cuts. Five girls would be going home tonight, a swarm of emotions interrupting their sleep because they hadn't made the team. Their egos would be crushed, their feelings hurt. They would have to face the rest of the student body knowing that they weren't as good as the ten girls who would remain. The ten girls who made the cut would be Carver's newest, freshest dance team.

My palms began to sweat as I sat on the bleachers next to Tameka, awaiting my destiny. My eyes glanced across the gym and found a pair of light brown ones staring my way. Marcus Carter rested his chin in the palm of his hand. He smiled when he caught me looking. Why was he there? To humiliate me? I rolled my eyes.

As the edited version of 50 Cent's "Disco Inferno" rang through the gym, I started making moves that I had practiced all summer with Jade. My yellow and gray FILAs hitting the hardwoods at a consistent pace, my hips moving to a similar rhythm. When I danced, I went to another place; another world—all the faces in the gym became nonexistent as I did my thing. For two whole minutes, I allowed the music to consume my entire body. And then, something happened—the most horrible thing that would threaten to ruin my life. I tripped over my shoestring that had come untied with all the movement.

Embarrassment rushed across my face, and I wanted to cry. And as my legs began to stiffen, the music continued to play. I continued to dance, as Miss Martin made notes on her clipboard. Surely she was handing me demerits for my clumsiness. I would be one of the five sleepless girls who'd be cut from the team; my worst nightmare. My mind went to Jade, as 50 Cent's voice rang through the speakers in the gym. I'd blown it for both of us.

I sat through the rest of the routines, but couldn't wait until it was over. As soon as the last girl finished performing, and Miss Martin gave her spiel, I threw my backpack across my shoulder and rushed though the glass doors. I couldn't breathe and needed some air. Couldn't believe I had screwed up my chance of making the team. Any mistake would be an automatic elimination, considering the talent of all the girls in there. I searched the line of cars for my father's truck. He was nowhere in sight, and I wondered where he could be at a time like this, when I had a rush of tears that needed to be released. I pulled my cell phone out to call home.

"Where's Daddy?" I asked my mother.

"Indi, he's stuck in traffic. He left you a message on your cell phone. Didn't you get it?"

"No, ma'am," I said. "I haven't even checked my messages."

"He doesn't know when he'll get there," she said. "I would come and get you myself, but you know my car's in the shop."

"So what am I supposed to do?" I asked, my voice on the verge of cracking.

"You'll have to wait for your father," she said. "Are you okay?"

"I'm fine."

"You don't sound fine," she said. "How did tryouts go?"

"Okay," I said reluctantly.

"Did you dance to Twenty-five Cent's song?"

"It's 50 Cent, Mama."

"Twenty-five Cents, Fifty Cents. Whatever, Indi."

"Yes, I danced to his song," I said softly. "Ma, I need to go so I can wait for Daddy. I'll tell you about tryouts when I get home."

"Okay, Indi. He should be there shortly."

I couldn't wait to hang up as I stood in the courtyard. The leaves on the trees were blowing about, restlessly. Students stood around chatting and waiting for their parents, while the cross-country team passed by, jogging at a slow pace. In the distance, I heard a whistle from the football coach in the field behind the school.

"You need a ride?" I heard a deep voice in my ear.

"My daddy's coming," I said and kept my back to Marcus.

"You were still good." He laughed. "Even after you tripped over your shoestring."

"You think it's funny?" I turned to face him, his light brown eyes glistening in the sunshine. His dimples were nice, too, as he smiled.

"I don't mean to laugh," he said, "but if you could've seen your face…"

"I hate you," I said and stormed off.

He caught up with me again.

"I'm sorry, girl. I was just playing."

I ignored him, and did my best to keep the tears from falling. But they did anyway, and before I knew it they were burning the side of my face. I wiped them away with the back of my hand. Marcus wrapped his arms around me. I wanted to punch him in his face and tell him to get away from me, but I actually found comfort there, my face buried in his chest. His cologne pleasing to my nose.

"Look, I was just playing, Indigo," he said. "You're a better dancer than all those girls put together."

I looked up into his light brown eyes to see if he was serious. He wasn't smiling.

"Well, it doesn't really matter now, does it?" I asked, not really expecting an answer. I pulled away from his embrace.

"You think that just because you tripped over your shoestring, it means you can't dance?"

"No, it means I won't make the team," I told him. "I know that the competition was tough, and all Miss Martin needed was five girls to eliminate."

"True that," he said, "but if she got any sense, she knows that stuff happens. And she'll judge you based on the talent that she saw in you the first time."

I looked into his eyes again. He was serious.

"Although it *was* crazy funny when you tripped." He laughed again. "I wanted to bust out laughing right there in the gym."

"I can't stand you!" I said, and rolled my eyes.

"Everybody in the gym wanted to laugh," he said. "Not just me."

When I saw my father's truck pull up, I was grateful.

"You are so stupid." I left him standing there. "I don't even know why I told you anything!"

"I'm sorry," he said.

I kept moving.

Even if I didn't make the team, his words would still ring in my head forever, *you're a better dancer than all those girls put together.*

He was so right!

chapter 7

Marcus

when I pulled up in front of the house, my pop's Dodge pickup was in the driveway, the backside of it propped up with a jack, the tire lying in the grass. My pop's legs were stretched out from underneath the truck. He was under there doing something with tools.

"Hey, Pop," I said, and he slid out from underneath the truck, oil covering his face and hands.

"Hi, son." He pulled himself up, stood, grabbed an old rag and wiped his hands with it. "You forgot to take the trash out this morning."

I had been in a hurry that morning and forgot all about the fact that it was trash day.

"I forgot, Pop. I'm sorry."

"You don't have many chores, Marcus, but that's one of them. And I expect you to do it," he said. "Gloria had a hissy fit. You know how she can get."

"I know," I said. "But I was just rushing to get to school."

"Try not to forget again. She had to pull that trash can out to the curb herself." He almost had a smirk on his face when he said it. I wanted to crack up laughing at the thought of Princess Gloria pulling that stinking can out of the garage and setting it on the curb all by herself. That would've been a nice sight. I hate I missed it.

"I won't forget again."

"How was school, son?" he asked.

"It was cool," I said. "I'm thinking about playing football again."

"That's good. I know how much you like football. And you're good at it."

"Yeah, but I haven't decided how it fits into my Master Plan yet, though."

"This Master Plan of yours, I really wish you would let go of it. You need to be thinking about taking over the family business after high school."

"Pop, I'm not trying to..."

"Marcus, your grandfather built this business, and then passed it on to me. And I'm trying to teach you the ropes, so I can pass it on to you someday."

"Pop, I want to go to college, and I'm working toward a full scholarship. I'm not interested in buying, selling or managing real estate, or sitting around being somebody's landlord," I told him. "And you should think about hiring somebody to manage those properties for you, so you don't have to run around town collecting rent...doing repairs..."

"Son, I run around town collecting rent and doing repairs because I want to stay connected with my tenants. I've known these people for years, and it's not just about collecting rent. It's about building relationships. Some of them are even friends."

"I know, Pop. That's real cool. I can appreciate that, but it's just not for me."

"Well, it is today, because I need for you to take me over to East Point to help this young lady unclog her toilet. As you can see, my truck is not running, so I need for you to drive me."

"Can't you just take the keys to my Jeep and go?"

"No, I can't. But I am going to take a shower, and when I get done I'll be ready to go."

"Yes, sir," I mumbled, threw my backpack across my shoulder and hustled up to my room.

I pushed the play button on my CD player, as Jamie Foxx's voice rang through my speakers, and Kanye West began rapping on his "Gold Digger" track. I pumped it up loud enough for it to bounce off the walls in my room, but not too loud. Didn't want Gloria complaining, which was what she did best. I dropped my backpack in the middle of the floor and fell facedown onto my bed. I listened to the music, and took it all in. My cell phone vibrated in the pocket of my jeans, but I ignored it. Whoever it was would have to leave a message. I needed few minutes to myself. It stopped vibrating and then started again, so I pulled it out of my pocket. Checked the number. Didn't recognize it, and didn't answer. After the same number flashed on the screen a third time, I figured it must be important. I answered.

"Hello."

"Hi, Marcus," the voice said. "You know who this is?"

"No, I don't."

"You must give a lot of girls your number, then."

"Not that many," I said, and then sat up in bed. "Who is this?"

"This is Charmaine."

"Charmaine who?"

"From Mrs. Murray's class, Marcus. Stop playing."

"Oh, yeah, you sit by the window." I remembered the girl who wasn't very cute, but she was a cheerleader. And she'd practically begged for my number, so what could I say? "What's up?"

"You got a date for the homecoming dance?"

The homecoming dance. Just then, I thought about Indigo. I kept meaning to ask her, but every time I got around her, I forgot what it was I wanted to say. She had that sort of effect on me. I happened to glance out my bedroom window and peeped into hers, which was right across the yard. There she was, pacing the floor in her bedroom, yapping away on her cell phone. I wondered who she was talking to.

"Well?" Charmaine was asking.

"Well, what?"

"Do you have a date or what?"

"Yep, I'm already taking somebody."

"Who?" She asked.

"Indigo Summer."

"Indigo Summer?" she asked with an attitude, as if I had said a curse word. "Indigo Summer is going to the dance with her boyfriend, Quincy Rawlins."

I almost dropped the phone. She had a boyfriend? And it was Quincy Rawlins?

I wanted to say, "I just saw him yesterday under the bleachers after football practice hugging all up on Angela Miller." But I didn't. I just said, "I know she has a boyfriend. I was just playing."

I got up and walked over to the window. Indigo was still yapping on her phone. She caught me watching, and snatched her blinds shut.

"So you wanna go with me or what?" Charmaine was asking.

"Yeah," I said, halfway listening to her. "I'll go with you."

"Cool. I'll tell my mama to take me to the mall to get a dress," she said. "I gotta go, Marcus. I'll see you in class tomorrow."

"Alright," I said, and glanced over at Indigo's window again.

Quincy Rawlins? What did she see in him?

Pop tuned my radio station to Atlanta's oldies station, 104.1. I hated when he rode in the car with me, because he always controlled the radio. It was either the oldies station or smooth jazz. Either way, it drove me crazy. But I never complained, I just dealt with it, and hoped that the ride would end soon.

"Turn left here, Marcus," he told me. "It's the yellow house up here on the right."

I pulled into the driveway of one of Pop's rental units. A little boy rode his bike on the sidewalk in front of the house.

"My mama's in the house," he said to us, as we both stepped out of my Jeep.

Pop grabbed his tools from the backseat and I headed for the front porch.

"How you doing, Rufus?" A young slender woman stepped outside onto the porch. A light blue dress hugged her figure. "I'm so glad you could come."

"No problem, Beverly," Pop said. "This is my son, Marcus."

"Hello, Marcus. I've heard so much about you." She smiled and reached her hand out to me. I took it in a handshake. "That's my little boy, Justin." She pointed toward the boy on the bike. "Justin, come here."

"I can't right now, Mama, I'm about to pop a wheelie."

"Boy, you betta come here," she said, with her hands on her hips.

After her tone of voice changed, Justin immediately dropped his bike and ran toward the front porch.

"Say hello to Mr. Rufus."

"Hello, Mr. Rufus," Justin said.

"And this is Marcus." She pointed to me. "Say hi."

"Hi," Justin said.

"Hey, Justin, what's up?" I asked.

"Nothing," he said, and then took off running, and jumped back onto his bike.

"That boy is so full of energy. I wish he would devote that much energy to his schoolwork. Especially math. He's flunking math."

"Oh, that's too bad," Pop said, as we followed Beverly into her house. "Maybe Marcus could help him out a little bit. He's a whiz in math."

I wanted to shut Pop up. He was always volunteering me for stuff.

"That would be so nice, Marcus," Beverly said. "Could you take a look at his math homework and make sure he did it right?"

"Yes, ma'am," I said reluctantly, not really feeling this whole trip. Couldn't understand why Pop didn't just hire someone to unclog toilets and fix pipes and such, instead of running all over town doing it himself, and then dragging me along for the ride.

Pop headed for Beverly's bathroom to unclog her toilet. Beverly disappeared into a back bedroom and came back with Justin's math book in her hand. She handed it to me.

"Here it is, Marcus. You can just have a seat right here on the sofa while you look it over," she said. "Can I get you something to drink? I have Coke and grape soda."

"I'll take Coke," I told her, and then found a seat on the dull, brown sofa that seemed to sink down in the middle.

I opened Justin's workbook and began reviewing his math problems. Over half of them were wrong, and when I told Beverly so, she called Justin into the house.

"Now you sit right down there next to Marcus, and he'll tell you what you did wrong."

Justin plopped down on the sofa next to me, and I went over his math problems with him.

"Look, man, this is the deal. When you subtract big numbers like this, you have to make sure you reduce."

"Reduce?"

"Yeah, let me show you." I worked through the problems with him one by one and tried to make him understand.

Told him what he did wrong, and how to do them correctly. He listened, erased the wrong answers and changed them to the correct ones.

"You understand now?" I asked, after we worked through each problem.

"Yep. Now that you walked me through it, I understand," he said, "but when my teacher tells me, or my mom tells me, it doesn't make sense."

"Well, just remember what I said, and you'll be okay."

"Okay, Marcus," he said. "Can you come help me with my homework tomorrow?"

"I don't know about tomorrow, little man, but…"

"Can you come by a couple of times a week, Marcus, and help him?" Beverly asked before I could finish my sentence. "I really would appreciate it. And I will pay you."

"Of course he can," Pop said, coming out of the bathroom with his tools. "He'll be happy to help out."

"Can you, Marcus?" Justin was bouncing up and down. "Please?"

"Okay, yeah, I can come by, maybe next week sometime and help you out."

"Thank you," Beverly said, smiling. "And thank you for fixing my toilet, Rufus."

"No problem," Pop said. "Let's go, Marcus."

I stood and followed Pop out the door.

"It was nice to meet you, Miss Beverly," I said. "I'll see you next week, Justin."

"Bye, Marcus," he said, and held on to to his mother's hand as Pop and I climbed into my Jeep.

The day hadn't been a total loss. At least I helped some kid learn math, and that made me feel good. That made me feel real good. As Pop tuned my radio to the oldies station, some tune by the Temptations rang through the speakers. Pop sang along as we drove home with the windows down catching a cool breeze.

After I loaded the dishwasher with dishes, and swept the kitchen floor, I rushed upstairs to my room. Hopped in the shower, tuned my radio to *The Quiet Storm* on V-103 and hit the sack.

chapter 8

Indigo

I actually fell asleep on the bus, and didn't wake up until the huge tires had brushed against the curb. I'd spent half the night talking to Quincy on the phone, and the other half sweating the dance team tryouts. When the bus driver opened the door, kids started knocking each other over to get off. As I stepped off, I spotted Quincy across the courtyard, and just as I was about to tell him to "wait up," Patrice Robinson grabbed him by the arm and rested her head on his shoulder. What did she think she was doing? What's worse is he didn't seem to mind. He wrapped his arm around her shoulders and they walked into the building. I lagged behind, my backpack thrown across my shoulder, and my lip poked out.

"You wait until I see him," I mumbled, as I made my way to my locker.

"Hey, Indi!" Tameka shouted, "Wait up."

I waited for her to catch up.

"We have to go see if we made the team," she said, and pulled me along.

She led me toward the cafeteria. A crowd of people gathered around the list that was posted on the wall. We pushed our way up to the front of the crowd, past the chatter and chaos. Tameka stood in front of the list, her finger scrolling along. I covered my eyes, too afraid to look.

"Tameka Brown." She spotted her name and sang. "Hey..."

"I can't look," I said, my eyes still shut.

"I don't see your name, Indi," she said. "Hmmm...I don't know...if you made it...let me look again."

I took my hand from my face, walked up toward the list. I had to know. Took my finger and slowly scrolled through the list of names, my heart pounding so loud I could hear it. INDIGO SUMMER. There it was again, my name in bold letters on the page. When I heard a scream, I thought it had come from my mouth, but realized it was Tameka.

"We made it!" she said, and we both started jumping up and down.

She started doing a dance in the hallway, and I followed along. Before long, the crowd started dancing, too, humming an imaginary tune until one of the teachers broke it up and told us all to go to class. Reluctantly, we did so.

"I'll see you at dance practice after school, Indi," Tameka said, heading toward her locker, which was in the opposite direction of mine. "Congratulations, girl, we did it!"

"Yes, we did," I said, smiling from ear to ear.

I couldn't wait to tell Jade. I had accomplished it for both of us.

Quincy was standing at my locker when I got there.

"Congratulations, boo," he said, and kissed my cheek. When there was no spark in my eyes, he leaned back and asked, "What's wrong?"

"Nothing," I said. Didn't want to ruin my good news, by bringing up stupid stuff. Besides, there was probably nothing to Patrice's hanging all over him. Girls were always sweating the football players. And he was on the starting lineup, for crying out loud. Why wouldn't girls be hanging all over him? As long as they knew who his girlfriend was, what difference did it make? And once people saw us together at the Homecoming Dance, they would all know. "Just walk me to my class."

"Heard you made the dance team, girl." He smiled, and my heart melted. "I don't know if I can walk next to you, since you a star and everything."

"Please." I punched him in the shoulder. "You're the star. Got girls hanging all over you and stuff."

"What girls?"

"I saw you with Patrice Robinson this morning."

"Patrice?" He frowned. "She's just my play cousin. Her mama knows my mama."

"Oh."

"That's why you were acting all funny a few minutes ago?"

"Something like that," I said, pulling my math book out of my locker, and then slamming my locker shut.

"Don't start tripping, girl," he said, and then grabbed me in a semi-headlock. "Lots of girls like me, but I'm with you. Remember?"

"Yeah, I remember," I said.

"Then don't start trippin'. I can have any girl I want in this school, but I chose you."

"I know," I said.

But that green-eyed monster, called "jealousy," would probably rear its ugly head again. Going out with a boy like Quincy, I was sure of it.

Instead of practicing a routine, we did squats and exercises with our legs. I was confused; I thought this was a dance team. But we weren't dancing, we were exercising. If I wanted to exercise, I would've tried out for the basketball or volleyball team. Kristal must've been thinking the same thing, because she raised her hand and asked Miss Martin the question that was lingering on the tip of my tongue.

"What's up with the exercises? I thought this was a dance team," she said.

"This is a dance team," Miss Martin informed her.

"Well why are we working out like we're playing sports or something?" Kristal went on to ask.

"You don't think dancing is a sport?"

"Well...I don't know..." Kristal stumbled. "I guess it is."

"It absolutely is," Miss Martin said, and I was glad I hadn't asked the question, because Miss Martin suddenly got an attitude. "If you have a problem with strengthening your legs before dancing, you're free to leave."

"I'm cool with it," Kristal said.

"Anybody else got a problem with the way I conduct dance practice?" Miss Martin looked around at all the faces in the gym. Girls who were grateful just to be on the team. We weren't about to mess that up.

"No," we all said in unison.

"Good," she said. "Now give me ten more squats."

After several sets of squats, we practiced our routine for the upcoming event, which happened to be halftime at the Homecoming game. It would be our first performance as a team, and we didn't have much time to practice. Miss Martin blew her whistle and we lined up in the center of the floor of the gym. When she asked us to team up with a partner, Tameka and I chose each other. Tameka was beginning to fill the void that Jade had left when she moved away. She was funny and had me laughing all through practice. And even though she lived in another part of town, and rode a different bus, we found ourselves trying to figure out how to get together that weekend.

"Ask your mama if you can spend this weekend at my house," she said after practice, "and then we can go to the mall on Saturday and find our dresses for the dance."

"I'll see. But my parents don't usually let me spend the night with people they don't know."

"Well beg them, and plead with them," she suggested. "Clean up your room first, and maybe they'll go for it."

"Now that might work," I said. "I'll ask and let you know."

"Cool."

"Who's taking you to the dance?" I asked.

"Jeff Donaldson," she said, wiping sweat from her forehead as we both headed outside to look for our parents. "He's on the football team with Quincy. They're friends. You've seen him. He's fine, tall, dark and muscular."

"Oh, yeah, I've seen them together," I told her.

"We've been going together for about a year now," she said, smiling. "He gave me this."

She held her hand out and showed me the silver promise ring on her finger.

"Ooh, that's pretty," I said. "What he give you that for?"

"It means that I'm his forever," she said. "We're getting married after college. He's going to Morehouse, and I'm going to Spelman so we can be right here in Atlanta together."

"You already know what college you're going to?"

"Yep," she said. "We have it all planned out."

"Girl, I haven't even thought about the college I'm going to. Senior year seems so far away, especially when you're just a freshman."

"You should still be thinking about what you wanna do, Indi. It'll be here before you know it. And you need to start competing for scholarships and stuff as early as next year."

"Please, I just wanna enjoy being a freshman right now, have a real boyfriend, and be on the dance team. College is definitely a goal, but I can't think about that right now. I'm struggling just to find where my classes are in this big ol' school."

"Cool. Don't think about it, then," she said, spotting her mother's black BMW and heading toward it. "You just think about practicing them moves we learned at practice today. And don't forget to ask your parents if you can spend the weekend."

"I will," I said. "I'll call you tonight and let you know."

"Okay, but don't call until after *106th and Park* goes off, and *America's Next Top Model.* I have to see which one of them fake females is going home tonight."

"My money is on Furonda," I yelled. "She's the next one to go."

"We'll see," she said, and then climbed into her mother's car.

As my daddy's pickup pulled up next to the curb, I had to smile. I had a new friend. She wasn't Jade, but she was just as cool.

chapter 9

Indigo

MY mama pulled her Chevy Cavalier into the subdivision filled with beautiful brick houses and perfectly manicured lawns. I thought about asking her if we could park our car around the corner and walk the rest of the way to Tameka's house, but I knew she wouldn't go for it. Her car was making all sorts of noises that made me want to crawl into the backseat, and cover my head up. All that time at the repair shop, and it still sounded like it needed to be repaired. And no doubt it could use a new paint job. It was nothing like the BMW that Tameka's mom drove. On top of all that, I wished my mama could've chosen a better outfit than the old denim dress she had on; the one that she'd had since I was in kindergarten. I was embarrassed as Tameka's mother opened the front door.

She was tall and slender, and wore low-cut sexy

jeans, and a top that showed a whole lot of cleavage. She looked too young to have a teenage daughter.

"Come on in," she said. "I'm Melanie. But everybody just calls me Mel."

Mama and I stepped inside. Their house was beautifully decorated, with warm colorful walls and expensive-looking African art. Although our house was nice and clean, it wasn't this new and definitely not this beautiful.

"If you don't mind, please take your shoes off," Mel said.

Mama and I dropped our shoes at the door before sinking our feet into their snow-white carpet.

"I'm Carolyn." Mama held her hand out to shake Mel's.

"Glad to meet you, Carolyn," Mel said, and then turned to me. "I've heard so much about you, Indi. Tameka can't stop talking about you. Said you can dance your little fanny off. Is that true?"

"I'm alright." I blushed.

"I heard you did your routine to 50 Cent's 'Disco Inferno,'" she said. "Tameka said it was off the chain! You'll have to show me that routine."

I was in awe that Mel knew enough about 50 Cent to say his name right first of all, and her slang was impeccable.

Tameka appeared, carrying two bottles of Fruitopia. She handed me one.

"Hello, Mrs. Summer. I'm Tameka." She reached for my mother's hand.

Mama took her hand, and I could tell she was impressed with her manners. "Nice to meet you, Tameka. I've heard a lot about you."

"Nice to meet you, too," she said. "Mommy, can I show Indi my room?"

"Yes, if it's alright with Carolyn." We all looked at my mother.

"Can I stay, Mama?" I asked.

It had already been established that her decision about me spending the night would be made after, and only after she'd met Tameka and her mother.

"I suppose so," she said. "But you better behave and mind your manners."

I knew what that meant and always made sure I didn't make people think I didn't have any home training. "Don't embarrass me" is what Mama's words meant.

"Come on, let's go," Tameka said, and I followed her up a flight of stairs on the backside of the kitchen and down a long hallway to her bedroom, my tube socks making a squishing noise in the carpet.

Her room was decorated in pinks and whites, and posters of Bobby Valentino, Pretty Ricky and

Omarion were plastered on the walls. Her full-sized canopy bed was neatly made, and her closet was so full of clothes and shoes that the door wouldn't even shut. She closed her bedroom door behind us and pressed the power button on her CD player.

"What you wanna hear?" she asked, and fell backwards onto her bed. "I have all the latest CDs...everything!"

"I like rap," I said, and started looking through her stacks of CDs.

"I have everything by Snoop, Kanye West, 50... everybody..." she said. "My dad's a producer."

"Really?"

"Yep, he's at the studio right now," she said. "He works with a lot of local talent, and some famous people, too."

"You have Ludacris?"

She hit a button on the remote that controlled the CD player and Ludacris's voice rang through the speakers.

"I like some stuff by Luda," she said. "But I'm not much into rap."

"Who do you like?"

"Usher, Omarion...Omarion is so cute!" She laughed.

"He's alright," I said. "But what about Nelly?"

"He's definitely a hottie," she said. "But I don't

know very many girls our age who like hard-core rap, Indi. I mean, I like some rap."

"Well, I'm not like many girls our age," I said. "Everybody's different. That's what makes us all unique. If everybody liked the same stuff, how boring would that be?"

"I guess you're right," she said. "I don't like all the cussin', though."

"I don't either. I just listen to the edited versions," I told her, and then lay across her bed. "I like dancing to rap mostly."

"I guess." She smiled, and walked over to the window. "Your mom's leaving."

"Really?"

"Yep. I guess it's official that you get to spend the night," she said. "You wanna go to the mall now?"

"Yep."

It seemed that everybody from the south side of Atlanta had decided to visit Southlake Mall at the same time on Saturday afternoon. As we sifted through tables filled with underwear at Victoria's Secret, I suddenly missed Jade. Missed our Saturdays at the mall. From sunup to sundown, we used to shop until we dropped. Window shopped, that is, because most of the time we were broke. The money we did manage to squeeze out of our parents, was used for a bite to eat at the food court, a CD, a shirt, or occasionally, a pair of jeans, and not the designer ones. We didn't care about having money; it was fun just hanging out together. I missed Jade, but Tameka was just as fun. Even though our music tastes were different, we had lots of other things in common; like clothes, boys and a warped sense of humor.

We stopped at the nail shop for French manicures and pedicures, grabbed a bite to eat at the food court, and then hung around for a little while just checking out the crowd. We recognized many faces from school, and giggled as somebody's mama passed by with a head full of pink and green plastic rollers.

"Somebody forgot to tell her that you don't come out of the house like that." Tameka laughed. "And especially come to the mall on a Saturday afternoon."

"All she needs now is a pair of house slippers."

"And a bathrobe," Tameka said.

"Glad it ain't my mama," I said.

"I second that," Tameka said. "Your mom seems nice, by the way."

"She's okay. She's really overprotective. And my daddy, too," I said. "But your mother seems really cool. And she looks really young, too."

"She is young," Tameka said. "She had me when she was sixteen."

"That is young," I said.

"My dad is only two years older. They got married

when they found out my mom was pregnant," Tameka said. "Mommy had to drop out of school to raise me. And even though she went back for her GED, she never got to go to college. That's why I have to go...for both of us."

"And that's why you already got your college all picked out."

"That's right." She smiled. "Spelman won't know what to do when Tameka Brown walks through those doors."

"I hear you. But wouldn't you rather go away to school? Somewhere like UCLA or FAMU?"

"No, I need to be near Jeff, and he's going to Morehouse right here in Atlanta," Tameka said, and then changed the subject. "Come on, let's go over to Macy's and find us some dresses."

We shopped the Macy's clearance rack for dresses that would transform us into supermodels, like Eva, America's Next Top Model or Tyra Banks. We tried on at least ten dresses each, strutting in front of the mirror as if we were on the runway. Finally settling on the dresses that we wanted, Tameka called her mother to pick us up.

Mel pulled up in front of Sears, an Alicia Keys CD being pumped up. Tameka hopped in the backseat and I followed. Snapped our seat belts as she drove us to Applebee's for dinner.

"Order anything you want on the menu, girls," Mel said, and then told the waitress to bring her a margarita.

"Mommy, do you have to have a drink today?" Tameka asked.

"It's just a margarita, Tameka," she said. "I always get a margarita when I come to Applebee's. You know that."

"But we have company today," Tameka pleaded.

"I don't mind," I said, not wanting to cause any problems.

"Do your parents drink, Indi?" Mel asked.

"Sometimes they have wine with dinner," I said. "And sometimes my daddy has a beer when he's watching the football game."

"See, Tameka, Indi's parents drink, too."

"You're missing the point, Mommy."

"Then what is your point, baby?"

"Never mind," Tameka said, standing. "I have to go to the restroom. Can you just order me the chicken fingers basket?"

She slid from the booth and headed for the ladies' room. I peeled the wrapping from my straw and stuck the straw into my glass of Coke.

"Tameka gets so motherly sometimes," Mel said.

"She wants to make a good impression on you, Indi. She likes you a lot, and she doesn't have that many friends."

"I like her, too," I said. "And my best friend moved away at the beginning of the summer. I don't really have that many friends either."

"Then you two should get along just fine."

The waitress placed the margarita in front of Mel. "Here you go, ma'am."

"You know what, sweetie? I changed my mind about the margarita," she said to the waitress. "Can you just bring me whatever this young lady is drinking?"

"A Coke?" the waitress asked.

"A Coke sounds good," she said, and then smiled at me. A cappuccino-colored woman, Mel was very pretty. She wore natural-colored eye shadow, and had relaxed shoulder-length hair. She and Tameka would look like twins, except Tameka's hair was longer and she had a rounder face.

I smiled back.

The waitress disappeared.

"Now tell me about this boy, Quincy," she said.

I was shocked that she even knew about him. Tameka seemed to share everything with her mother.

"He's on the football team," I told her. "Linebacker."

"Hmm, linebacker. You like him?"

"I haven't spent much time with him. We just started going together last week."

"Well, you just make sure he treats you nice, or you drop him like a bad habit," she said. "You hear?"

"Yes, ma'am."

"You don't take no crap off of him," she said. "And he is not to touch your pocketbook until you're ready."

"My pocketbook?"

Tameka slid into the booth, back from the restroom. "Mommy, why are we talking about pocketbooks?"

"I told Indi that Quincy is not to touch hers until she's ready." Mel took a sip of her Coke.

"What's a pocketbook?" I asked.

"You know...your goodies," Tameka tried to explain, and looked at me with one eyebrow raised.

I still didn't get it.

"You're not to have sex with him until you're ready," Mel said.

"Ohhh," I said and then giggled.

Tameka started giggling, too, but Mel wasn't laughing.

With a serious look on her face, she leaned forward and said, "These little nappy-headed boys only want one thing, and you can't just give it to them because they ask. Just remember that."

"Okay," I said, afraid that if I said anything different, she might pull her belt off and rip it across my behind right there at Applebee's.

"Mommy, you're drinking Coke. What happened to your margarita?"

"They ran out of margarita mix," Mel said, and then winked at me.

I winked back.

She was nothing like my mother, who would never carry on a conversation about boys and my pocketbook. My mother, Carolyn Summer, avoided conversations like that. But Mel was open and direct, just like my Nana Summer. And I liked her.

chapter 10

Indigo

"Indi, you sleep?"

"No, I'm awake."

As the moonlight brushed across her face, I could see the whites of Tameka's eyes staring at me, her head resting in the palm of her hand, as she balanced herself on her elbow.

"Have you ever done it before?"

"No," I answered softly. "You?"

"Not yet."

"Not yet? Which means that you're considering it?"

"Everyone's doing it, Indi. I think we're the last two teenagers on earth who haven't."

"Really?" This caused me to sit up in the twin bed.

"Yes," she said.

"What about what your mom said about our pocketbooks?" I asked her.

"Jeff said that if two people love each other, then it's not wrong." She smiled and I could see her pearly whites in the moonlight.

"So you love Jeff?"

"He's so sweet, Indi," she said, her eyes all glassy. "I think I do love him. No, I'm pretty sure I do."

"Does he love you, too?"

"Of course, silly." She fell onto her back, her eyes facing the ceiling. "Why else would he give me a ring?"

"Yeah, you're right. I guess he does love you." I fell flat onto my back, and stared at the ceiling, too. Began to wonder if I would ever love someone, or if someone would ever love me enough to give me a ring. Would Quincy ever feel the same way about me that Jeff felt about Tameka? I had never given love much thought until now. But love still seemed so complicated, because it seemed to come with other stuff, like jealousy, hurt and most of all, sex. And sex was not something that thrilled me. I couldn't understand what all the hype was about. Maybe someday I would, I thought as my eyes became heavy. But right now, I didn't.

"Just wait until you and Quincy fall in love."

Now that was something I'd never considered. I didn't foresee that happening, but I didn't say that to Tameka. Instead, I just allowed my eyes to give in to sleep that I was suddenly fighting.

"You sleep, Indi?" Tameka asked again. And this time I didn't answer. The bed had already pulled my body in and soon I was dreaming.

As I turned over and adjusted myself across the bed, I could've sworn I caught the smell of smoked sausage. I opened one eye, and adjusted it to the sunlight as Tameka, dressed in her Victoria-Secret pajamas with PINK written across her behind in huge white letters, opened the blinds. Loud gospel music shook the entire house. They were songs I recognized because our choir at church sang them just about every Sunday.

"Hey, sleepyhead, it's about time you woke up."

"Is it morning?" It seemed that I'd just shut my eyes for the night.

"Of course it is."

"What time is it?" I asked, opening both eyes.

"Nine-thirty," she said, and snatched the covers off of my tired body. "My mama cooked breakfast. She said for us to come downstairs and eat."

"Y'all don't go to church?" I asked, and had packed a dress in my bag for Sunday School, just in case.

"Naw. My mama just plays the gospel music real loud and we play like we at church." Tameka laughed.

"Oh, okay," I said and didn't hesitate to jump up, run to the bathroom and wash my face.

* * *

Fat smoked sausages, pancakes and scrambled eggs were on the kitchen table, along with a pitcher of orange juice and two glasses of milk. The kitchen was bright, with plenty of sunlight beaming in through the windows. There seemed to be a million windows in the kitchen, and there was an island in the center of the floor. Not like the traditional kitchen at my house.

"Well, good morning!" Mel said. "Did you get enough sleep, honey?"

"Yes, ma'am."

"Have a seat and dig in." She grinned, pulling her short, sexy robe tighter as she flipped pancakes on a griddle.

I took the closest seat at the end of the table, took a sip of milk. Tameka plopped down in the chair next to mine. Sunday's *Atlanta Journal-Constitution*, the local newspaper, was scattered about on the table.

"I want three pancakes, Mommy," she said, taking a drink of her milk, creating a milk mustache on her upper lip.

"How many would you like, Indi?" Mel asked.

"I'll take two," I said.

"Then two it is." Mel touched my nose with her fingertip. "Your mother said she would be here to pick you up after church, so make sure you get your stuff together after you eat."

"Yes, ma'am," I said, and patiently awaited my hot, golden pancakes.

It was always more fun at someone else's house than it was at home, and I soon realized that as I bounced my overnight bag onto the bed in Tameka's room. I began packing my clothes and got a little depressed about having to go home. It was interesting to learn how other families did things, especially when they did things differently than what you were accustomed to. I sat on the edge of my bed, peered out the window and waited for my mama to pull into the driveway.

When I got home, I raced to my room and shut the door. It wasn't that I didn't want to spend time with my parents, but conversations with Tameka left me with a lot to think about. Conversations about love and sex and boys. It was all racing through my mind like a freight train. If we were the last two teenagers on earth who hadn't had sex, then what was wrong with us?

My blinds were open and I caught a glimpse of Marcus pacing the floor in his room, his headphones covering his ears, a chicken leg in his hand. He caught me watching him and blew me a kiss. I rolled my eyes at him, and snatched my blinds shut. Why did boys have to be so stupid?

chapter 11

Marcus

I pulled into the driveway, Killer on the passenger seat, his head hanging out the window. As soon as I stopped my Jeep, he started barking uncontrollably.

"Shut up, dude!" I told him, and he whimpered and sat on his hind legs. Cocked his head to the side and gave me a look as if to say, "what did I do?" German Shepherds had a way of communicating with you. They had their own personalities, and I knew what he was thinking at all times. Sometimes they acted just like little kids.

I hopped out of my truck, and Killer hopped out behind me. Justin spotted me and started pedaling his bike toward me at full speed.

"Marcus!" he yelled, but stopped dead in his tracks at the sight of Killer.

I recognized the fear in his eyes and said, "He won't hurt you, little man."

Killer ran toward Justin, jumped up on him and knocked him off of his bike. Justin yelled. "Stop!"

"He just trying to play with you, man." I laughed. "Killer! Leave him alone."

He continued to jump up on Jason.

"Killer, sit!" I yelled once more, this time in a deep voice that let him know that I wasn't playing.

At the sound of my voice, Killer moved away from Justin and innocently rubbed up against my leg. "Stop playing so much, dude." I rubbed his head and he began to whimper like a child again.

"I'm scared of him, Marcus. He's so big."

"He won't hurt you, man. He's just a puppy." I continued to rub Killer's head.

"A puppy?" Justin's eyes grew big.

"Yeah, he's just big for his age." I laughed. "He just wants you to play with him. Here, rub his head like this."

Justin reached his hand out reluctantly toward Killer's head. Rubbed the top of it, smoothing his golden mane.

"Here, rub him under here, too," I said, telling Justin to rub Killer under his chin, just the way he liked it.

Slowly, he touched Killer under his chin.

"See he won't hurt you, little man. He likes

that," I said. "He wasn't trying to hurt you, he just wanted to play."

Justin began to relax and so did Killer.

"Why you call him Killer?" he asked.

"Because if he doesn't like you, he's trained to attack."

"Has he ever attacked somebody, Marcus?"

"Just a mailman once." I laughed. "He likes just about everybody, though."

After Justin let his guard down, he and Killer started running around the yard. Justin would run just to see if he would chase him, and of course he did. Then Justin would throw a tennis ball, and Killer would take off after it, bringing it back and dropping it at Justin's feet. Justin would throw it again, and Killer would fetch. They were okay after that.

"Hey there, Marcus." Beverly held the door opened, a silk scarf wrapped around her head.

"Hi, Miss Beverly," I said.

"That your dog?" She asked, and I nodded. "He bite?"

"No, ma'am. He's harmless." I smiled. "He's still a baby."

"That big old dog is just a baby?" she asked, stepping out onto the porch to get a better look at Killer. "How old?"

"Seven months," I told her. "Shepherds grow fast."

"I suppose so," she said. "You care for something to eat? I fried some chicken."

"That sounds really tempting, but my stepmother, Gloria, gets really upset if I don't eat at home. She thinks I don't like her cooking."

"Do you?"

"I can't stand her cooking." Beverly and I both laughed.

"Well, your daddy loves to eat. How he end up with a woman who can't cook?" She laughed harder.

"I don't know, Miss Beverly."

"Well, you can eat here and at home." She smiled. "Just one piece won't hurt a thing."

Beverly disappeared into the house, the place where those wonderful mouth-watering smells were coming from. You could smell the seasonings a block away, and I couldn't wait to sink my teeth into a piece of that fried chicken. Gloria never fried chicken; said that it was unhealthy and claimed that it was the reason that black folks died from high blood pressure. She baked everything in the oven; chicken, fish, even French fries. Everything! I was sure that from time to time, my pop wished he could go back to his New Orleans roots just for a day and taste some of those Cajun seasonings that he grew up on. My grandmother and mother deep-fried everything. Even the turkey on Thanksgiving was deep-fried.

"Can we take Killer for a walk, Marcus?" Justin asked.

"We need to get started on your homework first, little man. That's why I'm here. To help you out."

"I know, but can we just go for a quick walk?"

"Work first, and then we play," I said. "Now go get your math book, so we can get started. If it's not too late when we're finished, we'll take Killer for a walk."

"Aw, man."

"Don't get mad. We have to get the important stuff out of the way first." I sounded like my pop. I guess he was rubbing off on me.

Justin ran into the house to grab his math book, almost knocking his mother over as she opened the door carrying a piping hot chicken leg wrapped in a paper towel. Handed it to me.

"Here you go, Marcus." She smiled. "And there's plenty more where that came from."

"Thank you."

Justin and I sat side by side in the rocker on the porch. He opened his math book, handed me his worksheet.

"This is what we had to do today. Problems one through eight. And they were hard, too."

I scanned the worksheet to make sure Justin had worked the problems correctly. Got distracted as three cute girls walked past the house, giggling and talking loud. Girls were always exaggerating their actions, laughing when there was nothing really that funny, and trying to be seen when boys were around.

"Hey, Sasha," Beverly yelled to the cappuccino-colored girl with shoulder-length brown hair.

"Hi, Miss Beverly." The girl waved. "Hey, Justin."

"Hey." Justin barely opened his mouth, as he looked up at her.

She was cute, and I couldn't stop staring.

"Come here, Sasha, I got somebody I want you to meet," Beverly said.

She walked toward the porch as her friends waited at the curb. As she got closer, I got a better look at her light brown eyes and perfectly white teeth.

"Hey, sweetie pie." Sasha pinched Justin's cheek, and he looked embarrassed.

He was blushing like crazy and trying to play it off. It was obvious he had a crush on her. Reminded me of the crush I once had on Mrs. Banks, my fifth grade teacher. She was so fine. She would squeeze my cheeks and tell me how cute I was. She didn't know it, but I had secretly made her my girlfriend.

"Oh, he's trying to act shy," Beverly said. "Why you trying to act shy in front of Sasha, Justin?"

He shrugged his shoulders. I knew! Because he thought she was hot.

"Well, we both know that he's not." Sasha smiled, and that's when I noticed her cute little dimples.

"Sasha, this is Marcus. He's Justin's tutor," Beverly said. "Marcus, Sasha watches Justin for me in the evenings until I can get home from work. She watches him for me sometimes on the weekend too."

"How you doing? Nice to meet you," I said.

"You, too," she said. "You go to Douglas?"

"George Washington Carver."

"Oh. Our football team is playing y'all next Saturday. Homecoming game."

"I know." I smiled. "And we plan on winning, too."

"I doubt it. Carver sucks," she said. "You play football?"

"No."

"What grade you in?"

"Tenth," I said, and felt like I was being sized up. "What about you?"

"I'm in the eleventh," she boasted. An older woman, I thought.

Killer raised up and rubbed up against Sasha's leg. I guess he knew quality when he saw it. She didn't flinch, just started rubbing him underneath his chin. She wasn't scared of him like most people were when they first met Killer. He usually scared the crap out of everyone, especially girls. The only other girl who wasn't scared of Killer was Indigo. When he barked at her, she told him shut up before she knocked his teeth out. That only made me more attracted to her. A girl who could play basketball in the middle of the street with a bunch of guys and talk junk to a German Shepherd like that was not an ordinary girl. She was extraordinary.

I wondered if Sasha could play ball as I checked out her smooth legs. There weren't any muscles in her legs like in Indigo's. Indigo's legs looked as if she did squats every day. They were strong and muscular.

"He likes her," Justin said.

I wanted to tell him that I did, too, but I played it cool. I turned my attention back to Justin's homework.

"Well, I gotta go," she said, bouncing back down the stairs. "I'll see you tomorrow Justin."

"Okay," Justin said.

"Nice to meet you, Marcus," she said to me, and then joined her friends who were waiting at the curb.

I watched as they walked to the corner and then turned down the next block. Watched until I could no longer see them.

Tutoring Justin might not be that bad after all, I thought.

chapter 12

Indigo

Butterflies floated around in my stomach, each flying in different directions as I sat on the front porch. Dressed in a soft pink, sleeveless dress trimmed in lace, my hair pulled into a mass on my head, eyeliner, lipstick and mascara on my face, I waited for my date. He was already thirty minutes late, and I was becoming nervous. My parents kept snapping pictures and staring at me with these goofy smiles on their faces. At one point, Mama even had tears in her eyes.

"It's just a Homecoming Dance," I told them. "It's not that serious."

"It is serious. It's your first real date, Indi," Mama said, wiping tears from her eyes.

My father wouldn't let me date until I was fifteen, so I guess this was a milestone moment in my life. The first time a boy ever came to my house and picked me up and my parents were more excited than I was.

I heard Marcus's front door creak and watched as he stepped out of his house and onto his porch. His tie undone, he rushed to his Jeep. He looked my way and waved. I waved back.

"What's up?" he yelled, looking extra handsome in a black tuxedo, lavender cummerbund and shiny black shoes. I wondered who he was taking to the dance, and almost asked, but didn't want him to think I was prying, or that I cared.

"Nothing," I said to him, and managed a smile. His smile was beautiful and calming and warm, even caused my butterflies to settle.

"You waiting on Quincy?"

"Yep."

"He's a little late, ain't he?" he asked, and looked at his watch.

"He's on his way," I shot back, not wanting him to know that I had already assessed the situation and wasn't pleased at all.

"You look very pretty, Indi. I hope Quincy makes it here soon," he said and rushed to his Jeep. Jumped in and pulled off down the block.

"Me, too," I whispered to myself.

As a navy blue Nissan Maxima slowed in front of the house, my butterflies started flying rapidly again.

My stomach churned as Quincy stepped out of the driver's seat wearing a black tuxedo with a pink cummerbund that matched my dress, no tie and pink-and-white Nikes. His hair was trimmed perfectly, and he carried a white corsage in a plastic container that he had probably picked up at Publix grocery store on the way over.

"Hi, Indi. Sorry I'm late," he said as he climbed onto our porch.

"Hi, Quincy," I said, and suddenly Daddy appeared behind me.

"Hello, sir," Quincy said, grabbing my father's hand in a strong handshake. I was relieved to know that he at least had manners.

That was important because I knew that Daddy would judge him based on whether or not he seemed to have home training. That would determine whether or not he could come back again. So I was relieved.

"How are you, son?" Daddy said. "Running a little late aren't you?"

"Yes, sir, and I'm sorry. I had an errand to run for my mother."

Just then, Mama rushed out onto the porch carrying one of her old shawls. One like the old ladies wore at our church.

"Here, Indi. Take this. You might get cold later and you can throw this around your arms."

I took it, but had no intentions of wearing it tonight or any other night. It was too old fashioned for my taste, but I didn't want to hurt her feelings.

"Hello, young man," Mama said and shook Quincy's hand.

"How you doing, Mrs. Summer?" Quincy asked. "It's very nice to meet you."

"What time can we expect her home?" Daddy asked.

"What time would you like her home?" Quincy asked.

"No later than twelve-thirty," Daddy said.

"Twelve-thirty, Daddy? We won't even have time to get anything to eat," I protested. "One-thirty?"

"One o'clock, Indi. And that's final."

"I'll have her home by one, sir." Quincy stepped in, and then took the corsage out of its package. Pinned it on me, and I was embarrassed as his hand accidentally swept across my breast. He was obviously experienced at this stuff; pinning corsages on girls, because he did it perfectly. How many times had he taken somebody to a formal dance?

"Y'all look so nice. Stand over there so I can take a picture," Mama said, digital camera in hand.

"They wearing sneakers to formal dances now?" Daddy got a better view of Quincy's shoes.

"It's the style, Daddy." Quincy and I both laughed.

"Times sure have changed since I was in high school."

"Yes, they have," I said, blinded by the flash from the camera. "Can we go now?"

"Y'all have a good time." Mama kissed my cheek. "I'll make sure your nana gets copies of these pictures. She'll be so excited. Wouldn't you like to call her before you leave, just to say hello?"

"Mama, we're already running late." Quincy and I started down the stairs. "I'll call her later."

"You have your cell phone, Indi?" Mama asked.

"Yes, ma'am."

"Call us if you need us, baby," she said.

"Okay."

Quincy opened the passenger door of his mama's car, and I hopped inside. Couldn't wait to get away from those parents of mine; the ones who still treated me like a five-year-old. At some point they would have to let go. As soon as we got to the end of my street, Quincy pumped up a single by Dem Franchize Boyz, "Lean Wit It, Rock Wit It," the unedited version. That nice, mannerable young man who had just stepped onto my parent's porch for the first time had disappeared by the time we reached the corner.

"You look fine, girl," he said.

"Thanks. So do you." I was tense. Clasped my hands together with nervous energy.

"You can loosen up. We're away from your parents. It's just you and me now. So just relax and kick back."

"Okay," I said, but the butterflies wouldn't keep still, as he did about eighty miles an hour in a residential area.

The school's cafeteria had been transformed into a ballroom with streamers, colorful balloons everywhere, and fluorescent lights throughout the room. In one corner of the room, a DJ played booty-shaking music and in the opposite corner, Coach Robinson served cake and punch to a long line of students. I immediately lost Quincy to his boys from the football team as they huddled together in the middle of the floor, flexing and showing off their tuxedos. I was left against the wall by myself, looking around to see who all was there. A few people were on the dance floor getting their grooves on. As I scanned the room checking out all the different dresses I prayed that no one had mine on. Someone covered my eyes from behind.

"It's about time you got here." Tameka smiled, her strapless red dress covering every inch of her round hips. Her body was fully developed like a grown woman's—like her mother, Mel's. She had it all in the right places, unlike me. Mine was divided sparingly—a little bit of hips here, a little bit of booty, some nice muscular legs—thanks to the squats that Miss Martin demanded from the dance team—but not much in the breast department at all. Some girls received it a lot slower than others.

"That dress is off da hook, girl!" I said. "It looks so much better than it did when you tried it on at Macy's."

Tameka modeled her dress in front of me, twisting and turning as if she was on the runway. "You look really cute yourself."

"Thank you."

As the DJ played "Shoulder Lean," Tameka pulled my arm. "Come on, let's go get our men so we can dance."

Tameka broke up their little party, grabbed Jeff by the arm and I grabbed Quincy. We led them to the dance floor. Quincy started doing a dance called the Shoulder Lean and I followed. Tameka and Jeff danced to our right. Across the room and to my left, I spotted Marcus dancing with Charmaine Jackson, his date for the evening. They were color coordinated. His eyes met mine, and he smiled. I smiled back. I wondered how the two of them ended up together. She definitely wasn't his type, and she wasn't even cute. Had she asked him, or had he asked her to the dance? What did I care? He was just my stupid next-door neighbor anyway.

chapter 13

Marcus

For some reason, I couldn't keep my eyes off of Indigo. And she was definitely wearing that dress. She wasn't overdeveloped like some of the other girls in the place, but she had a little something that was worth looking at. She was perfectly built, in my opinion. And the moment I saw her walk in with Quincy Rawlins, my blood started to boil. Jealousy rushed through my veins. He didn't deserve a girl like that. He was one of the biggest dogs at our school, and it was always the dogs that got first dibs on the girls. The good girls. Not girls like my date, Charmaine Jackson, who hadn't stopped talking since the moment I picked her up at her run-down apartment complex.

Her brothers had stood outside in their sagging pants and bandanas wrapped around their heads, throwing up gang signs as I pulled into the parking lot. Her mother had answered the door wearing a short, sheer nightgown and asked me if I could run to the store and pick her up a package of cigarettes.

"A package of Kool Milds, baby," she'd said. "And pick me up one of them disposable cameras so I can take you and Charmaine's picture."

"Ma'am, I'm not old enough to buy cigarettes," I told her. "I'm only sixteen."

"Ma'am? Don't be calling me no ma'am! You can just call me Shirley," she said. "And you can just tell James down at the CVS that the cigarettes is for me. He'll sell 'em to you."

She pulled a wad of cash out of her purse and handed me a ten-dollar bill.

"Miss Jackson, I really don't feel comfortable buying cigarettes," I told her.

"Oh, never mind, boy. I'll get one of these no-good sons of mine to run to the store. Y'all go on to the dance, and have a good time."

I was relieved to finally jump in my Jeep and burn rubber out of the parking lot.

chapter 14

Indigo

I stood on the wall nursing a cup of punch, as everyone was on the dance floor, sweaty from all the movement. On Quincy's way back from the rest-room, he stopped and whispered something in Patrice Robinson's ear and she smiled at him. Before long the two of them were on the dance floor, his hands wrapped around her body and hers exploring his chest. I was fighting mad. How could he bring me to a dance and then dance with someone else? This time I wouldn't be so calm.

"Why you standing over here by yourself?" Marcus had found his way next to me, and I was actually happy to hear his voice in my ear.

"Waiting for Quincy to get done dancing with that tramp over there."

"Who, Patrice?" he asked, as if he hadn't noticed.

Everybody in the place noticed how they danced with each other.

"Yes, Patrice."

"There's one of two things you can do about that." He smiled and it was the first time I noticed how beautiful his smile was. And he smelled so good. "You can either go over there and tell him that you don't appreciate him dancing with her..."

"What's the other thing?"

"You can come out here and dance with me, let me show you some moves."

"Where's your date?"

"Her girls came and whisked her off somewhere to go gossip."

We both laughed.

"How did you end up with her anyway, Marcus? She's not even your type."

"My type?" He smiled that smile again. "What's my type?"

"I don't know. But it's definitely not Charmaine Jackson. Rumor has it that she has given it up to everybody on the football team."

"Really? I hadn't heard that one." He shrugged his shoulders. "I needed a date, and I had run out of options. The person I wanted to invite was already taken."

"And who was that?" I asked.

"Just some girl I know."

"Do I know her?"

"I don't know. You might," he said. "Can I get a dance or what? Or do you plan to just hold up the wall for the rest of the night?"

Without another word, he pulled me out onto the dance floor, and I didn't resist. Marcus drew me close, and I actually felt comfortable in his arms—sort of protected. I rested my head on his chest as we swayed to the sound of Jamie Foxx's "Play a Love Song."

"How did a girl like you end up with a guy like Quincy?" He asked.

"What kind of question is that?"

"A simple one," he said. "You're much too beautiful for him. He's a dog."

"You don't even know him like that."

"See that's where you're wrong. I have known Quincy a long time, Indi. Since we were in grade school together, we both have played football in leagues all over the city together. He ain't about jack."

"You're jealous of him."

"Jealous?" he asked.

"Yes." I smiled. "Just because your date didn't work out, now you trying to spoil mine."

"Right. I'm jealous of Quincy Rawlins." He laughed. "I'll just let you find out for yourself."

"Cool. You do that."

"But I'll be here when you're ready to talk," he said. "Because I think you're special, Indigo Summer. I think you're very special."

"I admit. We got off to a bad start, Marcus. Maybe we should try and be friends. I think that's what this is all about."

"That's not what this is about, but I would be happy to be your friend, Indigo," he said. "Does that mean we can hang out a little bit?"

"Hang out like where?"

"Like at the mall, or a football game…go to a movie?"

"Maybe the mall or a football game or something." I smiled. "But I don't know about a movie. I do have a boyfriend, you know."

"That's right. How could I forget that?" he asked.

There was suddenly silence between us for a moment, a very uncomfortable silence. I needed to say something that would lighten the mood. "Where did Mr. Davis get that suit?"

Marcus laughed. "Probably Goodwill."

We began to people-watch and laugh about some of the stuff they were wearing. We laughed at the light blue suit Mr. Davis wore; it looked as if he'd owned it back in the sixties. We cracked on Miss Goodman's two-toned shoes that didn't match anything she had on. I actually enjoyed the few moments I spent with

Marcus. He had a sense of humor and he was fun to talk to. I was sorry that I hadn't given him the time of day before. As Quincy's eyes met mine, I gave him a little wave.

"He's looking over here." I smiled as the look of envy flashed across Quincy's face when he spotted me dancing with Marcus. "Hug me closer."

Marcus did as I asked until the song finally ended.

"You ready to go, Indi?" Quincy asked, giving Marcus an evil eye as he approached.

"Whenever you are."

"If we're going to grab something to eat, we better get going. You know what your father said," he said. "I wanna make sure I get you home on time."

He grabbed my elbow and we headed toward the door.

"I'll catch you later, Indi," Marcus said.

"Okay," I said, and followed Quincy to his mama's Maxima.

As we approached the edge of the parking lot at school, Quincy turned out onto the street and then accelerated. We drove a few miles and to a nearby park. Quincy drove into the park, the gravel making a crushing noise under our tires. Although the sign read: NO ADMITTANCE AFTER HOURS, Quincy continued down the stretch of the path until we reached a parking area. He maneuvered the car into one of the spots.

"What are we doing here?"

"Got something I wanna show you."

"Thought we were getting something to eat?"

"I'm not that hungry. Are you?" He asked, and before I could answer, said, "Matter of fact, I'm not hungry at all."

He put a CD in, and adjusted the volume on the stereo.

The park was dark and almost eerie. The only light shining was that from the moon and the dashboard in Quincy's mama's car. I could barely see the whites of his eyes as he reclined in his seat and began caressing my face with his fingertips. When he leaned over and kissed me, I relaxed and gave in to his kiss. I loved the softness of his lips and his kisses usually tasted minty and fresh.

"Are you okay?" he whispered.

"Yes," I whispered back. Couldn't understand why we were both whispering. It wasn't like anyone else was around.

As his tongue swirled to the roof of my mouth, his hand began to probe, making its way to my knee and then on up to my thigh. My heart started pounding so loudly, I wondered if he could hear it. I liked kissing, but wasn't sure I was ready for much more than that. I thought about Mel and how she said not to let anybody in my pocketbook before I was ready. I took that to heart.

"Just relax, baby," Quincy said. "I won't hurt you."

"I'm not ready," I said.

"Yes, you are. You just need to relax, Indi."

Who was he to tell me what I was ready for? Only I could decide that…and had.

"I'm not ready," I said again, pulling his hand away and straightening my dress.

We hadn't even been dating that long. We hadn't even talked about sex. Hadn't talked about the fact that I was still virgin and wanted my first time to be special. With someone that I cared about. We hadn't talked about the consequences of sex, like HIV and other sexually transmitted diseases, or about pregnancy. I didn't even know if he planned on using protection or if he had any.

Quincy rested his head on the back of the leather driver's seat and stared straight ahead. He was frustrated. "When will you be ready?" he asked.

"I can't say for sure," I told him, and my heart wouldn't stop beating at the rapid pace it was pulsating. My hands shook as I snapped my seat belt on. "Can you just take me home?"

"Yep, I'll take you home," he said and snapped his seat belt on, too. Restarted the engine.

He was mad. I could tell.

But I didn't care. I knew what made me comfortable and what didn't, and this definitely did not.

When he pulled up in front of my house, I placed my hand on the door handle.

"Will you call me later?" I asked softly.

"Yeah, I'll call you later," he said, never looking my way. His eyes remained straight ahead. I expected him to at least lean over and kiss me goodnight, but he didn't.

I waited a few minutes, and then hopped out of the car. Made my way up my front steps and when I got to the door, I looked back at Quincy. He was watching me to make sure I got in, but pulled off the minute I stepped inside. My father was crashed out on the sofa in the family room. I tiptoed past him and made it to the stairwell. Just as my foot touched the bottom step, his voice rang out in the darkness.

"Did you have a good time?" he asked.

I crept back into the family room and stood in front of him.

"Hi, Daddy. I thought you were asleep."

"All closed eyes aren't sleep, baby," he said, and

peeped at his watch. "You're home earlier than curfew. What's going on?"

"Nothing."

"You okay?"

"I'm fine, Daddy."

"You don't look fine. What's on your mind?" He sat straight up and adjusted his position on the sofa. "Anything you wanna talk about?"

"No, Daddy. Everything's fine, I'm just tired," I said and rubbed my eyes. "Just want to go to bed."

This was definitely not a subject for my father. He wasn't ready for a heavy conversation such as this. Quincy would have a hit out on him before morning if my father knew the details of my evening. Daddy wasn't taking this whole dating thing very well as it was. After all, I was his baby girl.

My father sighed, cocked his head to the side and peered at me with those inquisitive eyes of his. In his heart of hearts he knew that something wasn't quite right, but he wasn't sure what. Fathers just knew.

"Well; I guess you should go on to bed then, baby. Got to get up for church in the morning," he said. "I'm turning in, too."

Daddy hit the power on the television set, followed me up the stairs, dressed in his light blue cotton pajamas and brown leather slippers that Nana Summer had given him for Christmas two years ago.

At the top of the stairs, I kissed his cheek and said, "Good night, Daddy."

"Good night, baby. I'll see you in the morning."

I rushed to my room and changed into my pajamas. Sat on the edge of the bed, thinking through the choices I'd made all night. Wondering if I'd made the right ones. Part of me wanted to cry as I caught a reflection of my face in the mirror. My makeup had begun to smear. I went into my bathroom, grabbed a washcloth and wet it. Cleaned the makeup from my face, and brushed my teeth.

Just as I was about to call it a night, I heard a light tap on my bedroom window; sounded like a small rock hitting it. And then another tap. When I opened my blinds, Marcus stood with his window wide opened and was about to throw another Skittle at my window.

"What are you doing?" I asked, as I pulled my window opened. I was actually grateful to see him. His face was like a breath of fresh air.

"I saw you coming home just now. That punk didn't even walk you to the door," he said, as his wife-beater hugged the muscles in his chest. "What took y'all so long? Where'd y'all go after the dance?"

"Nowhere special," I said. "Where did you and Charmaine go after the dance?"

"I took her to McDonald's and then dropped her behind off at home."

"Please tell me you didn't take her to Mickey D's."

"Naw. I took her to Applebee's, and then took her home. Her mama was having a party and asked me if I wanted to come in and play some dominoes. I told her I would pass." We both cracked up.

"What did she order at Applebee's?"

"A Bourbon Street steak with a loaded baked potato. And the heifer had the nerve to order an appetizer, too. I told her that what she needed to order was a salad with light dressing on the side."

"And she cussed you out, right?"

"No doubt." He laughed. "Ate her steak, appetizer and part of my meal, too."

"That's what you get," I said.

"That's what I get for what?"

"For taking a girl like Charmaine to the Homecoming Dance."

"Well, the girl that I wanted to take already had a date."

"And who was that?" I asked, hands on my hips.

"Nobody special. Just some freshman."

"Oh," I said, changing the subject. "You forgot to tell me what you ordered at Applebee's."

"Chicken fingers. Why?" he asked.

"Just asking."

"You forgot to tell me where you and Quincy went for dinner," he said.

"Umm..." I thought for a moment. Was Marcus a friend or foe? "I wasn't really that hungry, so we just went somewhere to talk."

"Oh," he said, his eyes staring into mine. Marcus was easy to talk to. "Did he try something?"

"No, we just talked," I lied.

"Well, you need to get some sleep. I'll holler at you tomorrow."

"Good night, Marcus."

"Sleep tight," he said, and then shut his window.

chapter 15

Marcus

I stood on the porch, ringing the bell as the hot Atlanta sun beamed down on my neck. On the other side of the door, I could hear the patter of feet rushing toward me. The door swung opened.

"Hey, Marcus. It's about time you got here," Justin said.

"What's up, little man?" I asked, and gave him a high five.

"My mama's not here," he said.

"You here by yourself?" I asked.

"Nope. Sasha's here," he said and frowned. "She won't let me go outside and ride my bike."

"Who's at the door, Justin?" Sasha asked and then appeared in the doorway. She was wearing a low-cut pair of jeans, a red cropped shirt and matching red-

and-white FILAs. Her microbraids were pulled back into a ponytail. "Oh. Hey, what's up, Marcus?"

"What's up?" I asked her and smiled. "I'm here to tutor Justin. Can I come in?"

"I guess so." She opened the door wider, and a strong smell of burnt popcorn brushed across my nose. "His mama know you're supposed to be here?"

"I come every week at the same time. She's usually home by now."

"She started a new part-time job and asked me if I could stay with Justin a little longer today." She smiled. "I guess you can come in."

"Thank you," I said and moved past her and into the living room. I took a seat on the sofa. Sasha's books were scattered all over the coffee table. "Did somebody burn some popcorn?"

"I left it in the microwave too long," she said and looked embarrassed.

"Oh," I said, and held my laughter inside. "Go get your books and stuff, little man. So we can get started."

Justin took off down the hall and to his room.

"Can I get you something to drink?" Sasha asked.

"Yeah. Some Kool-Aid would be nice."

"I'll be right back." She disappeared into the kitchen.

Justin rushed back into the living room and hopped onto the sofa next to me, opening up his math book and laying out his homework assignment. He grinned as he held up his math test. At the top of the page was a big red A plus and a smiling face.

"Check this out, Marcus!"

"Is that an A plus?"

"Yep!"

"Man, that's cool. Gimme some dap." He knew exactly what dap was and balled his hand into a fist. "You alright with me."

"What did he do?" Sasha asked, returning with an ice-cold glass of red Kool-Aid and handing it to me.

"He got an A plus on his exam," I said. "Show her."

He showed Sasha and she leaned over and kissed his cheek, then almost squeezed the life out of him. Justin blushed and then wiped all traces of her kiss away.

"You didn't tell me you got an A, Justin," she said. "Just for that, I might let you go outside and ride your bike later. That is if your mother's not here by the time you finish your homework."

"Alright!" he said. "We gotta hurry up, Marcus, 'cause I got some wheelies to pop."

"What you know about popping a wheelie?" I asked.

"I know a lot about it," he said. "Now come on, quit your yappin' and teach me some math."

"He's tripping," I said to Sasha and she started laughing.

I started explaining a few problems to Justin and then told him to work one out on his own. Told him to let me know once he'd completed it. Sasha had taken a seat in the chair across the room and started reading a book. She wasn't fully engaged in it, because I caught her checking me out a few times. She thought I wasn't watching, but I was; because I was checking her out, too.

"What you reading?" I asked her.

"*Native Son,*" she said, and held up the cover of the book for me to see it.

"Richard Wright?" I asked. "Good book."

"You read it?" she asked.

"Twice," I said. "What do you think of the main character, Bigger Thomas? Was he a product of his environment or a cold-blooded killer?"

"Both," she said. "What made you read it twice?"

"Just trying to figure out what was going through the brother's head. Trying to understand him better."

"And it took you two reads to do that?"

"Yep."

"So you understand him better now?" she asked sarcastically.

"A little better now."

"So do you believe that we all are products of our environment? That if we are raised in bad neighborhoods, then we will grow to be bad people?" she asked, sounding all intellectual.

"To some degree, but not totally. I believe we have

the freedom of choice. I can let my environment dictate to me who I can become, or I can become whatever I want in spite of where I live. In spite of the choices my parents made, in spite of everything." I was sharing my inner thoughts with this girl that I didn't even know. Stuff that I thought about all the time; stuff that had my mind racing in the middle of a geometry class when I should be paying attention.

"Marcus, you're a deep thinker," she said, and it was so nice to be able to talk to a girl who actually understood my thoughts. "What else do you think about?"

I didn't know if it was a trick question or what, but it was then that I decided to tell her about my Master Plan.

"I think about my Master Plan, and what I need to do to carry it out."

"Your Master Plan?"

"Yep," I said confidently. "It's the plan for my future."

"Okay," she said, and gave me a skeptical look. "Let's hear it."

"I had a teacher once tell me that because I'm black, I will never do anything spectacular, like go to an Ivy League college, or receive a scholarship in anything other than sports."

"He really said that?" her eyes grew big.

"In so many words."

"What did you say to him?"

"What can you say to someone that ignorant? You just have to prove them wrong."

"How will you do that?" Sasha asked, and I had her complete interest.

"That's what my Master Plan is all about. I absolutely have to maintain a 4.0 grade point average. I have to involve myself in my community and tutor kids like Justin here." I smiled at Justin, who was still struggling with the math problem I had assigned him. I playfully popped him upside his head. He looked up at me and frowned. "Sowing into him is like sowing into my own future."

"Marcus, you seem to have it all worked out." Sasha seemed like she was impressed, and her eyes softened as she stared at me with amazement.

"If you don't have a plan, you might as well just wander around like a traveler without a road map," I said. "What's your plan?"

"I'm going to a Georgia-based school, maybe Georgia State or the University of Georgia in Athens, so that I can get the Hope scholarship."

"Are your grades good?"

"I've been an honor roll student since the second grade."

"I could make the honor roll, too, if I could just get through math," Justin said. "It's my worst subject."

"It won't be for long, little man," I assured him. "You're going to be an expert in math when I get done with you."

"I'm done with my problem, Marcus," he said, and stuck the piece of paper in my face. "Here, look at it."

I grabbed it and worked through the problem in my head. His answer was correct, although he had arrived at the answer in a different way. I was pleased about that because that meant he was getting it. If he could work through it on his own, using his own way of getting to the answer, then that meant it was making sense.

"Yes!" I said and gave Justin a high five. "You are exactly right."

"Now can I go outside?" he asked.

"You have to ask Miss Sasha over there. She's the one who's responsible for you, dude."

"Can I, Sasha?"

"Okay, but I'll have to come outside and watch you."

Justin didn't hesitate to run to his room, wheel his dirt bike out the front door and down the few steps leading from the front porch. In just minutes, he'd hopped on it and was doing wheelies in the middle of the street.

Sasha and I sat on the rocker on the porch in the cool shade. Silent for a moment. I was feeling her. Not only was she cute and had a nice body, but she was smart, too. How often do you find that all wrapped up in a sixteen-year-old girl? Most girls have either one or the other going for them. They're either very cute and maybe have a nice body, but dumb as a doorknob. Then there are the girls who are smarter than me, but look like the bottom of my shoe. You rarely find the best of both worlds in one girl.

Indigo had a little of both. She was pretty and had a decent body, and her grades were decent. She had other stuff, too. She could dance. I'd seen her play basketball once in the middle of the street and she was actually pretty good at that, too. She had a sense of humor, and a way of making you feel small even when you thought you were all that. I liked Indigo, and for some reason, I couldn't get her out of my head. From the moment I saw her, I knew I wanted her. But she was taken. Taken by Quincy Rawlins, the biggest dog in school. I had to at least give it one more shot before I moved on.

Sasha was nice, too. She was beautiful, and had a nice body. She wasn't ghetto like Charmaine or some of the other girls I knew. She went to a different school, so I wouldn't have to worry about spending every hour of the day with her. She was smart, and easy to talk to. I hadn't dated anyone since Kim Porter, who broke up with me before I moved to the south side of town.

“You got a boyfriend?” I asked Sasha.

“Nope,” she said. “I talk to people, but nothing serious.”

“You wanna go to a movie or the football game sometime?” I asked.

“That’s cool,” she said, and gave me a smile with those beautiful dimples. “I’ll have to ask my daddy, though.”

“Let me know.”

Justin flew past the house, his arms stretched out wide.

“Look y’all, no hands!” he screamed, and then started laughing.

“I’ll race you, Justin!” Kevin, the little brown boy from across the street yelled, as Justin grabbed onto the handlebars again.

The two of them took off down the block at full speed, the nose of Justin’s bike just inches in front of his friend’s. Within minutes they were racing back up the block. They did this a couple of times and before I knew it, I heard a loud thump and Justin’s bike fell over and his head hit the pavement. He was crouched into a fetal-like position, holding onto his legs and moaning as if he was in excruciating pain.

Before I could think twice, I had jumped from the porch and sprinted toward him.

"What happened?" Sasha asked, running toward us. "I just turned my head for a second."

"What happened, little man?" I was standing over Justin, demanding an answer.

"It hurts so bad, Marcus. The pain is so bad," he said. "It's worse than before."

"Did you hurt your leg or something?" I asked.

"It's my joints." He moaned. "You have to call my mama. And I have to go to the hospital."

"Are you having a crisis, Marcus?" Sasha was standing next to me.

"Yes."

"A crisis?" I asked, still confused about the entire incident. "What's a crisis?"

"Justin has sickle cell, Marcus. We either need to drive him to the hospital or call for an ambulance."

I wanted to ask more about this sickle cell that had Justin on the ground moaning as if he was in great pain. Instinctively, I picked him up from the ground, and rushed him over to my Jeep. I gently placed him on the backseat. There was no time for calling an ambulance. They wouldn't get there quick enough.

"You comfortable, little man?" I asked as he lay crouched on my backseat.

He nodded a yes, but didn't look like it. His face was frowned and he was on the verge of tears. The only reason he hadn't started crying was because he was trying to be tough in front of me.

"It's okay to cry man, if you're hurting," I said and then hopped in the driver's seat. Sasha was already in the passenger's seat with her seat belt fastened, keeping an eye on Justin as I pulled out of the driveway.

My heart pounded as I flew through the streets of College Park. Sasha directed me to the hospital, as I was new to this part of town and unfamiliar.

"He goes to Egleston Children's Hospital, Marcus," she said and began trying to reach Beverly on her cell phone. "I have to call his mother and let her know what's going on."

"You have to tell me where Egleston is," I said. "I don't know where I'm going."

"Make a right here, Marcus," she said, and then left a message for Beverly on her cell phone. "She's not answering."

"You okay back there, little man?" I peered at Justin in the rearview mirror. Tears flooded his eyes and I wanted to cry myself.

At the circular drive just outside the emergency room, I put my Jeep in park. Rushed to the backseat, grabbed Justin and rushed him inside. Sasha was right behind me, and both of us called for help.

"Hey there, Justin." The nurse in rose-colored

scrubs, with a name tag which read Jennifer Smith, rushed over toward us. "You here again, little buddy?"

Justin nodded a yes to the nurse who knew him by name, and who had obviously treated him before. Just as quickly, an IV was placed in Justin's arm and he was whisked off and wheeled down a long hallway.

"Hi, I'm Jennifer Smith." The nurse held her hand out toward Sasha. "And you are?"

"I'm Sasha Jones, Justin's babysitter," she said.

"And I'm his tutor. Marcus Carter," I said and held my hand out to her as well. She grabbed it and I gave her a strong handshake.

"Nice to meet you both," she said, and then turned toward Sasha. "Where's Beverly, his mom?"

"I tried reaching her on the way over, but couldn't. I left her a message on her voice mail that we were here." Sasha was still shaken up. "I'll keep trying, though."

"Yep, you keep trying," Jennifer Smith said. "In the meantime, we're gonna get him started on some oxygen and help to ease his pain a little with some meds."

"What is this sickle cell that he has?" I had to ask. Everything had happened so fast, I was still in a whirlwind of emotions.

"Sickle cell anemia is a blood disorder that affects hemoglobin, which is a protein found in the red blood cells. Hemoglobin helps carry oxygen throughout the body."

"Yeah, I learned about that in my biology class," I told her.

"Well, sickle cell anemia occurs when an abnormal form of hemoglobin is produced, and causes the red blood cells to become odd-shaped or sickle-shaped and makes it harder for them to move freely throughout the body. You understand?"

"A little," Sasha said.

I just nodded.

"And instead of moving through the bloodstream easily, these sickle-shaped cells can clog the blood vessels and deprive the body's tissues of oxygen, making people who have sickle cell more tired and weak."

"Can you catch sickle cell from somebody?" Sasha asked, and I wanted to know the answer to that, too. After all, I had been spending quite a bit of time with Justin, and I was the one who had picked him up and put him in the backseat of my Jeep. I wondered if I would end up with sickle cell anemia before it was all over.

"No, honey. It's not contagious." Jennifer smiled. "You can't catch it from someone or pass it on to another person like a cold or something. People who have sickle cell anemia have inherited from their parents."

"So Justin's mom has it?" I asked.

"Beverly has the trait, and so does Justin's dad."

"He kept saying something about his joints aching. What's that about?"

"He's having what we call a crisis, where he is experiencing excruciating pain in his joints. What was he doing when he went into this crisis?"

"He was riding his bike," I said.

"Was he riding fast?"

"He was racing with the little boy across the street," Sasha said.

"He probably overexerted himself," Jennifer said.

"Will he be okay?" I asked.

"He's gonna be fine," Jennifer said and smiled. "Why don't you have a seat in the waiting room, guys. Grab a couple of hot chocolates, and continue to try and reach his mom. I'm gonna go check on Justin."

"Hey, tell him not to be scared. We're gonna wait right here until his mother comes," I told her.

"I'll be sure and tell him." She smiled and then disappeared.

After she walked away, I exhaled. This was way too much excitement for one day.

chapter 16

Marcus

Beverly rushed through the automatic doors in the emergency room; her Waffle House uniform held a million grease stains. Her eyes were bloodshot from the exhaustion of working two jobs as she searched the waiting room for familiar faces. She spotted us, as we sat there, sipping Styrofoam cups filled with hot chocolate and watching Seinfeld reruns on the television that hung in the corner of the room.

"Sasha!" she called and rushed toward us.

Sasha stood and her anxiety kicked in again.

"Miss Beverly. I don't know what happened. One minute Justin was riding his bike, and the next minute he was on the ground in pain." Sasha was almost in tears. "I was so scared. I didn't know what to do. I'm just glad that Marcus was there to drive him to the hospital, and..."

"Hey Marcus." Beverly turned to me, gave me a warm smile. "You drove him here?"

"Yes, ma'am."

"I appreciate that. Thank you." She touched my face with the palm of her hand. She was so calm, it was unbelievable. Sasha and I had been so scared and raised such a fuss, but Beverly kept her composure.

"I'm just glad I was there to help."

"I'm glad, too." She smiled. I could tell that she'd been through this before. She was unshaken. "I'm gonna go check on Justin. This usually takes most of the night and I know you both have school tomorrow. Have you called your parents?"

"I called my dad and told him where I was," Sasha said.

"I checked in with my pop, too," I said. I had called my father once the madness had settled down, and my heart had stopped pounding so fast.

"Good," Beverly said, and readjusted her worn purse on her shoulder. "Marcus, can you drive Sasha home?"

"Yes, ma'am, I can do that," I said.

"You sure you don't need us to stay?" Sasha asked.

"Yes, I'm sure." She smiled. "I've been through this with Justin a million times. Once the meds kick in and they get him comfortable, he'll be just fine. I'll call you both and let you know when he's out of the woods."

"Okay, cool. Because I need to know that he's alright," I said.

"I promise I'll call you."

"Good." I pulled my keys out of my pants pocket and turned to Sasha. "You ready?"

"Yeah," she said, and then hugged Beverly. "I hope Justin's okay."

"He'll be fine, honey," she said and then hugged me too. "Thanks again to both of you for getting him here."

"No thanks needed."

Before we could say our goodbyes, she had made a mad rush toward the nurse's station to find out which room they had Justin in. She looked over her shoulder at us and waved. That was our cue to go. We waved back and then exited through the automatic doors.

We were both quiet for most of the drive to Sasha's house. My thoughts were on Justin, and at one point I had even said a little prayer for him. He had really grown on me over the past few weeks, and I enjoyed tutoring him in math. He had become my little buddy. I often went home with a heavy heart, wishing Beverly had more money and could make ends meet a little better. I knew she was struggling just to keep food on the table for her and Justin. My plan was to drop by Kroger one day this week and buy her some groceries with my next paycheck. I had even scoped out Justin a pair of sneakers at the mall after I noticed the rundown ones he wore every time I saw him.

Beverly was a nice lady, always offering me something to eat whenever I tutored Justin. She even tried to pay me for my services once, but I refused to take it. Watching Justin's eyes brighten when he understood how to work through a problem, was payment enough. One night after tutoring Justin, Beverly handed me a brown paper bag. Said they were brownies loaded down with walnuts. She didn't know I had a soft spot for chocolate brownies. Inside the brown paper bag was a Ziploc baggie with three chocolate brownies inside. At the bottom of the bag, underneath the brownies, was a crumpled up twenty-dollar bill. I just smiled, and vowed that I would do something nice for Beverly and Justin. They both deserved it.

As I pulled up in front of Sasha's house, I glanced over at her. She'd fallen asleep and her head kept bouncing against the passenger's seat in my Jeep. I just watched her for a moment, and then gently grabbed her hand. She sat straight up, observed her surroundings, checked her mouth for drool and then looked at me.

"I fell asleep."

She wasn't telling me anything I didn't already know.

"You should wipe that slobber off your mouth."

She wiped her mouth with the back of her hand. "What slobber?" she asked.

"Right there," I said and ran my fingertips across her lips. I leaned in and soon my lips found hers. Her kiss was sweet and tender as we both closed our eyes and savored the moment. Her kiss tasted like the Now and Later that she'd popped into her mouth right after we left the hospital—sweet and strawberry-flavored.

"I hated what happened to Justin today, but I enjoyed being around you," she said.

"Same here." I had to admit, it felt good being with her. "I want to see you again. Can we go out on Friday night?"

"I can ask."

"Your daddy strict?"

Just then, the porch light popped on, and a middle-aged gentleman stepped outside wearing an old bathrobe that barely covered his middle-aged paunch. I knew about the paunch, because my pop had one. Sasha's father wore reading glasses and pushed them down on the tip of his nose, and peeked over the top of them to get a better look at the car parked in front of his house.

"I better go," Sasha said.

"Can I call you tonight?" I pulled my cell phone out of my pocket, ready to key her phone number in.

"It's best to e-mail me. Sashagirl at aol.com. I can't talk on the phone after ten on a school night," she said, and then opened the door. "I'll see you in cyberspace."

She hopped out of the car and rushed onto her front porch. Her father was saying something as they both went inside. The porch light went out, and then someone peeked through the blinds to see if I'd pulled off. I wondered if it was Sasha, catching one last glance at yours truly, or if it was her father, making sure I found my way off of his property. Either way, I pulled slowly from the curb and found my way home.

I crept into the kitchen, put the food away. Step-Mommy-Dearest had baked some chicken, cooked green beans with no real taste to them and had some other concoction I didn't recognize, sitting there on the stove untouched. I stuffed it all into the fridge and wiped down the counters. After loading the dishwasher and starting it, I peeked in on Pop who had fallen asleep in front of the television in the family room. I started to wake him, but knew he had an early morning. Instead, I pulled a blanket over him and then bounced up to my room. Opened the window and threw a Skittle at Indigo's window. It took me four throws before she drew her blinds and raised her window.

"It's about time you got home," she said.

"Were you waiting up?"

"No," she lied.

"Had a crisis tonight," I told her. "The little boy, Justin, that I've been tutoring got sick. He has sickle cell anemia and had an attack."

"An attack?"

"Yeah."

"Was it serious?"

"Serious enough to rush him to the emergency room."

"For real? Is he okay?"

"I hope so. His mama is supposed to call and let me know."

"I'll pray for him tonight," Indi said, her thick hair pushed back and wrapped in a silk scarf. She wasn't embarrassed about coming to the window with a scarf on her head either. That's what I liked about her. She wasn't afraid to be herself, unlike most girls. She was different. She didn't wear a lot of makeup and stuff, trying to be something she wasn't. She was still pretty, even with that rag on her head. She wore cotton pajamas with some cartoon character on the front of her shirt.

"What you been doing today?" I asked her.

"Went to the mall with Tameka."

"What did you buy me?"

"I didn't buy you nothin' with your ugly self." She smiled as she insulted me.

"Ugly?" I rubbed my palm across my face. "You call this face ugly?"

"Yes, I do."

"You better take a mental picture of it, so you can dream about it tonight." I laughed.

"Shut up, Marcus," she said. "Good night with your stupid self."

"Good night, Indi. Sleep tight."

She shut her window. I shut mine, too. Sat at my computer desk and turned on my computer. Logged onto my e-mail and saw that I had twenty-two new messages. Most of them were junk e-mails and I just went through and deleted them. Two of them were from a girl in London that I'd met online last summer. I'd never seen her in person, but she was nice to talk to. She had become my pen pal over the past year. Another e-mail was from my ex-girlfriend, Kim, asking me how I liked my new school. I hit the delete key. I hadn't spoken to her since she'd said, "let's just be friends," and the next day I saw her in the car with another dude.

One e-mail was from my mother, checking in to say hello. Said she was in San Diego on business and promised to pick me up a souvenir while she was there. I shot her a quick response and gave her my love, told her that I missed her. She immediately sent an IM, instant message, asking if I was interested in coming to live with her. How could she just IM me something like that, right out of the blue? IMs were for quick responses, but I didn't have a quick response to a question like that.

After Hurricane Katrina, the monster that had totally destroyed her home in New Orleans, Mom relocated to Houston and bought a condo there. She'd been living there for almost a year and said that once she got settled, she'd like for me to come and live with her. I didn't take her seriously. Thought she was just saying something in passing. Mom was always promising to send for me, or promising that she would come for a visit. But her job almost always came first. She never made good on her promises, and it only left me heartbroken in the end and took me too long to recover. I stopped putting my heart and soul into her promises; just took them with a grain of salt. I still loved her though.

When my parents were going through their divorce, I had to see a therapist to help me through my crisis. The therapist helped me to talk through what I was feeling. I was in a rage, because I felt as if my entire life had been turned upside down. And then in the midst of it all, Mom decided to drop me off at Pops one night, and then disappeared. Ended up in New Orleans with my grandparents. New

Orleans is where she'd grown up as a girl; it was her home. I remembered summers there with my grandparents when I was small. Granny would make her famous Creole dishes, like gumbo with the big, fat juicy shrimp, corn on the cob and sausages in it. She'd make jambalaya and we'd eat crawfish by the dozens. She could really cook, but she was the meanest woman in the world. Making me come inside before the streetlights came on, and if I didn't she'd pop me with a belt.

"Marcus, don't let dark hit you," she would always say. Which meant, don't stay outside playing after dark. "You be inside before the streetlights come on, you hear?"

I would always nod a yes, but miss curfew every time. Then I'd end up getting the beating of my life. Granddad was different. He was much nicer, and took me fishing a lot. We'd drive to Mississippi which wasn't that far from New Orleans, and fish in the Gulf of Mexico, sit on the bank with our poles launched into the water waiting for a bite. He'd tell me stories of when he was a boy, and have me laughing until my stomach hurt. Granddad was cool. That is, until he got Alzheimer's disease. Now he didn't even know my name. After the disaster, my grandparents moved to Mississippi and Mom moved to Houston.

Would love for you to come live with me now. What do you think? her IM said.

Her IM had caught me off guard. I hadn't really given Houston much thought when she'd mentioned the possibility months ago. Houston was a much better place to raise children, she'd said. Plus she missed me like crazy and couldn't wait to have me around again. I honestly didn't think she was serious; figured she enjoyed her life without me too much. This was definitely something I'd have to give some thought to. I responded.

I'll think about it and let you know.

Give it some serious thought, baby. You'll love Houston. There's a beach here, she said.

Really? That caught my attention. I loved the ocean. It brought back memories of Granddad and me at the Gulf of Mexico. I always loved going there, diving into the water in my trunks.

Why don't you come for a visit one weekend? You'll love it.

That sounds cool, I typed back.

Good. Let me know when and I'll buy an airline ticket.

I will, Mom.

Very good. Sweet dreams, babe. Get some rest.

Good night. Love you.

Love you, too, Marcus. At the end of her IM was an animated set of red lips as if she was sending me a kiss.

I logged out of instant messaging, and pulled my e-mail back up, created a new message for Sasha. Typed in her e-mail address, and in the body, I typed:

What's up? I really enjoyed spending time with you today. I know you're probably asleep by now, but wanted to send you a line anyway. Marcus.

Suddenly, an instant message popped up on the screen.

What took you so long? her IM read.

I responded I had chores and stuff to do.

Me 2. Plus my homework, she said.

UR cute, I typed, and ended my sentence with a smiling face. I didn't know where that came from, but suddenly felt the urge to tell her that.

UR cute too Marcus, but I have 2 go. I'll talk 2 U tomorrow.

Wait! Can I have your number? I typed it as fast as I could. Typing was never my strong point. Too many characters on a keyboard, and who had the patience to look for the right ones?

I waited for a response. Stared at the screen for five long minutes before realizing that she was gone. She had signed off and I had no way of reaching her again. I hated feeling helpless that way, but didn't have much of a choice. I'd have to wait for Sasha to get in touch with me. Who knew when that might be?

I shut down my computer, grabbed a hot shower, and brushed my teeth.

Before I drifted off to sleep, I asked God to keep an eye on my friend Justin for me. I didn't have many friends, but he was definitely one of them.

chapter 17

Indigo

It had been three days, one hour and forty minutes since I'd heard from Quincy. He hadn't called since dropping me off after the dance on Saturday night. His cell phone sent you straight into voice mail, and I'd already left six messages. He wasn't at school, and had missed two days of football practice. I was beginning to worry. My next option was to look up his home phone number in the white pages and call his mother, but I decided to give it another day. Maybe he'd call or at least send a text.

I sat at the dinner table with my parents, picking over my mashed potatoes all smothered in gravy, swearing to my parents that I was okay.

"You sure, Indi? Because you haven't touched a thing on your plate since you sat down. And you don't look good. You feelin' alright?"

"I'm fine, Ma," I said dryly. "Just got a lot on my mind."

"You haven't been quite right since that boy dropped you off the other night. You wanna talk about it?" Daddy asked.

"No, sir. I just wanna go to my room, if that's okay."

"Indi, I really would like for you to eat something," Mama said, and she was becoming really impatient with me.

"If she's not hungry, Carolyn, she's not hungry," Daddy said. "Don't force her to eat. Let her go on upstairs."

"Thanks, Daddy," I said, giving him a weak smile. My daddy was always there to rescue me, and I loved him for that. I made a mad dash for the kitchen to wrap my plate and stick it in the refrigerator for later. Felt guilty about leaving the dishes for my mother to load in the dishwasher, even though Nana Summer made me promise to help out more around the house. But tonight I just didn't have any motivation. She said that young ladies shouldn't have to be told what their responsibilities are. They should know what they are and do them. I had been so good about doing things without being told; cleaning my room, loading the dishes in the dishwasher after dinner, and vacuuming the family room on Saturday mornings, but tonight I just didn't have any energy to do anything. All I wanted to do was rush upstairs to my cell phone and see if I had any missed calls, voice mail or text messages from someone other than Jade or Tameka. How disappointing it was to have a message waiting, only to discover it was from one of my girlfriends, and not Quincy.

I opened up my flip phone and peered at the screen, and realized that I had two missed calls. Excitement rushed through me as I pressed the button to see who they were from. My heart thumped and I closed my eyes. Hoped with all my heart that it had been Quincy. Afraid that he'd moved on to someone else because I had said "no." There were so many girls my age who were willing to say "yes," that I was sure he'd found one. I thought of Mel's advice about keeping my pocketbook shut until I was ready. And Nana telling me how babies are made. That scared me to death. I even thought about the discussion we had in Sunday school about how God is not pleased when we don't practice abstinence. And I thought of my daddy's little talk that we had when I was in the seventh grade, about how easy girls give it up and good girls save it for later. All these thoughts had been rushing through my head, clouding my vision. Everything I'd been taught kicked in that night I was with Quincy, but honestly, I was starting to rethink that night. Something inside of me wished I hadn't listened to any of it. Saying "no" had caused me to feel isolated and left me with a broken heart. I was starting to wonder if I had made the right choice after all.

I checked the missed calls: one was from Tameka and one was from Jade. I threw the cell phone on my dresser and fell onto my bed facedown. I flipped over and then covered my head with my pillow; no television, no radio. I just wanted silence. And I had silence, except for the little tapping noise from Skittles hitting my window. Marcus. What did he want? He was the last person I wanted to talk to right now. I couldn't share the incident with him, because he would only tell me how it proves that Quincy really is no good. He would tell me that I should move on and that I deserved better. I tried to ignore the Skittles, but he wouldn't give. He obviously knew I was in my room. I jumped up, lifted my blinds and my window.

"What is it?" I asked impatiently, frowning. He grinned from ear to ear.

"Just seeing what you up to, In-di-go Summer." He enunciated every syllable of my first name.

"Nothing."

"You wanna go for a walk?"

"No."

"Come on, girl. I heard there's a fishing pond behind your house. I want to see it."

"It's just a little stupid creek, surrounded by a bunch of weeds."

"So? Let's go check it out anyway," he insisted. "Meet me outside in fifteen minutes."

Before I could protest, he'd already slammed his window shut and closed the blinds. Who did he think he was, barking orders at me like that? And what made him so sure I would show up? I didn't really feel like visiting that stupid old creek behind our house, the one where I'd lost my balance and fallen in when I was five years old, getting mud all over my new outfit. But anything was better than sitting in the house sulking. Besides, I liked talking to Marcus sometimes. He was really smart and made you think of life in a different way. Well, basically, he just made you think. Maybe, just maybe, he'd cheer me up.

As I stepped out of our air-conditioned house and into the Atlanta heat, it felt as if I'd stepped into an oven. Although the sun had gone down and dusk was just around the corner, it was still hot. I stepped off of my porch wearing a pair of khaki shorts, a pink Old Navy T-shirt and a pair of pink-and-white flip-flops. As I stepped into my backyard, I could see Marcus in the distance with his white wifebeater hugging his chest and a pair of oversized jeans hanging from his hips. He was carrying a huge stick and telling me to hurry up.

"I don't know why you wanna go down to this stupid creek," I yelled to him.

"I just wanna see what's down here," he said and took off down the hill, pushing tree branches and weeds out of the way like he was Tarzan or somebody.

I followed, wishing I'd changed into a pair of jeans, and noticing that the mosquitoes had already starting tearing into me. It was as if they'd been waiting all day for fresh meat to show up. And here I was. It didn't help that I was wearing an enticing fragrance that I'd picked up at Victoria Secret's the week before. It was a fragrance that obviously drove them crazy. I slapped my legs as the bugs seemed to attack me all at once. It was as if they were taking dibs on who could tear into the flesh the quickest.

"This is not cool, Marcus. The bugs are eating me up."

"Not to worry. I brought this." He pulled a can of OFF! out of his back pocket and held it in the air. "Come here, let me spray you down."

I stood there as Marcus sprayed OFF! all over my legs and arms. The spray was cold against my skin.

"That better?" he asked.

"I don't know yet." I frowned. "I don't like the outdoors. Or bugs!"

"Quit complaining, and come on," he said, and grabbed my hand.

He pulled me down the hill until we made it to the creek, a place where baby frogs and crickets made their homes. Who knows, maybe even snakes, too. Marcus stood over the water, trying to see what creatures might be hiding in there, while I stood off to the side, observing from a distance. He reached down into the water, wading with his hand. After a few moments a frog wriggled between his fingers.

"Yuck!" I screamed at the sight of it. "Put him back, Marcus!"

"Come here and say hello, Indi. He won't bite you." He laughed.

"You are so stupid. I'm out of here." I turned and briskly started walking back toward my house.

Before I got more than four feet away, Marcus's strong arms squeezed my waist from behind.

"Come back," he whispered in my ear. "I'm sorry."

I didn't pull away from his embrace. I actually felt safe, standing there all wrapped in his arms for a few minutes, taking in the smell of his cologne and the peppermint that he'd just popped into his mouth. It was perfectly natural for me to rest my head against his chest, and close my eyes. After a few moments, Marcus took my hand again and led me to a huge rock near the water. He sat down and invited me to sit next to him. I did. He picked up a few rocks and began tossing them into the water.

* * *

"I remember when you were in the second grade, with your ponytails flying in different directions on your head and you were snaggletooth."

"Snaggletooth?" I laughed. "What about those three-inch thick bifocals you used to wear? I bet you could've started a fire with them bad boys."

"What about those green-and-white plaid high waters you used to wear with that purple shirt?" he said, referring to an outfit that I had shed tears over when my mother gave it to the Salvation Army.

"I hated my mama for giving that outfit away. But what really ticked me off was when she threw my Raggedy Ann doll away," I told him. "Just because she was busting at the seams, she treated her like trash and threw her away. I cried for two weeks. Man, I would give anything to have a doll like that again."

"For real? Even now?" he asked.

"Even now," I said. "I've even searched for one like it, but they don't seem to make Raggedy Ann dolls anymore."

"That's serious."

"No. What's serious is those Power Rangers light-up shoes you used to wear," I said, and Marcus laughed so hard, there were tears in his eyes. He obviously remembered those shoes very well.

"You got me on that. I did have some Power Rangers light-up shoes," he said. "I loved them shoes, too. They were all that."

"I could tell, because you wore them every day." I laughed. "Even after the lights stopped flashing, you still wore them, like they were Nikes or something."

"They were the next best thing." He laughed. "You got me on that one, girl. It's okay though."

"Where did you go after second grade, Marcus? It was like you dropped off the face of the earth."

"My parents moved us to Stone Mountain that summer. We bought this big house, with a huge yard. They said that the schools were much better over there, and it was closer to my mother's job."

"Your mother seems nice. I saw her at the mailbox the other day. She smiled and said hello to me."

"Who Gloria? That's not my mother," he said. "That's my father's wife."

"Oh, she's your stepmother?" I asked.

"Something like that," he said.

"Where's your real mother?"

"She lives in Houston. Her and my father got a divorce about two years ago, and she ended up moving to New Orleans. After the hurricane she relocated to Houston. That's where she lives now." He threw another rock into the creek. "She wants me to come live with her."

"For real? You going?"

He shrugged. He seemed sad when he talked about his mother, and I looked for a way of changing the subject.

"What's up, Indi, you serious about this dude, Quincy?" he asked.

Up until then I'd forgotten all about Quincy and the fact that I hadn't heard from him in three days. Suddenly I was reminded of why I had been depressed.

"What is it that you see in him?"

"He's sweet. He's on the football team. He makes me laugh. He's popular," I said. "I have the guy that every girl at our school wants."

"He's a dog. He doesn't know how to treat a girl," he said. "You're too good for him, Indi."

"How come you don't like him, Marcus?"

"Because I know what he's about."

"And what's that?"

"He ain't about nothing!"

"Maybe you just have a crush on me yourself."

"Maybe I do," he said, catching me off guard. I expected him to deny it or tell me I was crazy. But he didn't. His eyes met mine and held them with his stare. "What you think about that?"

"I don't know." I shrugged my shoulders.

"I like you, Indi. I have liked you since the second grade."

"Why? I'm no different than any of the other girls out there."

"I think you're the most beautiful girl in the world." He was serious. "You should give me a chance to show you how a young lady is supposed to be treated."

"I can't. I'm Quincy's girl," I said, not really believing what I'd just said. How could I be somebody's girl when I hadn't even talked to him in three days?

"So, drop him."

"No."

"You giving it up?"

"Giving what up?" Did he really ask what I thought he asked?

"You know what I'm talking about. You giving it up to Quincy? Because that's all he's about," he said. "If you're not giving it up to him, he's moving on to something else."

"What about you, Marcus? Are you getting it from somewhere?" I asked, with attitude. He'd stepped on my toes with his line of questioning.

"I would never force a girl to do anything she didn't want to do."

"Are you saying that Quincy would?"

"Wouldn't he?" he asked, as if he already knew about what happened on Saturday night.

"I'm going inside." I stood, brushed the dirt from

the back of my shorts. "You don't know anything about me, or Quincy."

He stared into the creek. Threw another rock. I walked away slowly, hoping he'd stop me; run after me, but he didn't move. His back was to me. Another rock plopped into the water as I made it up the hill and to the side of my house. He never even turned around.

Marcus Carter didn't know anything about Indigo Summer.

As I searched my locker for my American history book, I felt strong arms wrap around my waist and the scent of Quincy's cologne dance across my nose. When I turned to face him, his haircut was fresh and he was grinning from ear to ear.

"What, you not happy to see me?" he asked.

"Where you been?" I asked, my hands on my hips. "I haven't heard from you in four days, Quincy."

"I been sick. Had some kind of stomach virus thing going on," he said. "My mother wouldn't let me come to school or talk on my phone. Or go to football practice."

"Are you over it?"

"Of course I'm over it." He smiled and reached into the pocket of his jeans. "I got you something."

"What?"

He pulled out a small purple box, handed it to me.

I opened it and held the silver necklace in the air. A big silver *I* dangled from the chain.

"You like it?" he asked and didn't hesitate to fasten it around my neck.

"Yeah, I like it." I smiled and then planted a kiss on Quincy's cheek.

"Cool," he said. "I'll see you after class then."

Before I knew it, he'd bounced down the hallway, turned to look at me. When he saw me checking him out, he blew me a kiss. I blew one back. Once he was out of sight, I slammed my locker shut, ran my fingertips across the chain. I hugged my history book and took my time getting to class.

I was still Quincy's girl after all.

chapter 18

Marcus

AS soon as the last school bell rang on Friday, I made a mad dash for the parking lot. The leather seats were scorching hot as I started the engine of my Jeep. I let the windows down and pumped up the air. Tuned my radio station to 107.9 and pumped it up. I received the news that Justin had been home for a few days and was feeling better, and I had plans of taking him to the mall to pick up a pair of those sneakers from Foot Locker. I couldn't wait to see his eyes light up right after I blessed him with a pair of the new LeBron Nike for kids. He would be the envy of all his classmates and have all the little girls in his class jocking him. The shoes would cost me half my paycheck, but it would be worth it just to see the look on his face. I had to beg Beverly to let him out of the house. She claimed that he was still weak and needed to rest. But after much convincing, she finally gave in. Said I could take Justin to the mall, to McDonald's for a Happy Meal, and then back home. So we were working on a tight schedule.

When I pulled into the driveway, Justin was in a chair on the porch, his legs swinging back and forth as he patiently waited for me. He wore a pair of cutoff shorts, a faded X-Men T-shirt and those same worn sneakers that he'd worn every time I'd seen him. He rushed to the car, and Beverly yelled at him through the screen door.

"Stop running, Justin!" she said and then shook her head. "Boy, you are too full of energy."

I waved to Beverly from my Jeep. There was no need of getting out because Justin was obviously in a hurry.

"I've been waiting for you all afternoon, Marcus," he said, a grin on his face from ear to ear as he climbed into the passenger's side. "What took you so long?"

"I had to go to school, dude."

"I know, but you got out at three-thirty. I started calculating the time as soon as three-thirty came around." He snapped his seat belt on. "I did a Mapquest from your school to my house, and it takes exactly fourteen minutes to get here. It took you twenty-five."

"I stopped for gas, man." I laughed. "And I had to say goodbye to a couple of the honeys before I left."

"Whatever, Marcus." He chuckled. "I can't wait to show you the shoes that I want. They are so tight."

"I already know which ones you want."

"But you don't know my style."

"What do you mean, I don't know your style? What's your style?"

"I have to look cool. I have a reputation to uphold, you know."

"I know, little man." I laughed. "You want McDonald's first or after we leave the mall?"

"Let's eat later."

I parked as close to Foot Locker as I could get, in order to save Justin from walking too far. He took off toward the double doors and I struggled to keep up. We headed straight for Foot Locker, and he zoomed in on the shoes that he wanted. It was a white, leather high-top sneaker sitting on the shelf just waiting for him. He picked it up.

"Here it is, Marcus," he said. "This boy in my class got some just like these."

"Why would you want shoes that somebody else already got?" I asked. "Get something different."

"But I like these."

The young salesman, who appeared to be about my age, approached and had overheard our conversation. He wore a black-and-white striped shirt, similar to one that a referee would wear, and the name Steve was plastered across his name tag. His haircut was tight, and I made a mental note to find out who his barber was. I hadn't found one on that side of town yet. He smiled and watched as Justin observed the shoe.

"If you like that shoe, I got one you might like even better, little man," Steve said, and handed Justin a black high-top sneaker. They looked similar to the ones Justin liked, but it was something a little better about them. "These just came in today. They cost a little more, but they are a nicer shoe."

"Whoa! Those are tight, Marcus." Justin grabbed the shoe from Steve.

"You like those?" I asked.

"Yep, Marcus. I like these better. Can I try it on?"

"What size do you need?" Steve asked, and looked at me.

I shrugged. I had no idea what size he wore.

"I need a one and a half," Justin said. "I think I still wear that size. It's been a long time since I had a new pair of shoes."

"I'll bring a couple of different sizes out. Just sit tight. I'll be right back." Steve disappeared into the back of the store.

"You sure those are the ones you like?" I asked, realizing that they cost a little more than I expected to spend.

"I like them a lot Marcus. But if you don't have enough money, I can get something cheaper."

"Naw, man, you get what you want."

When Steve came back, Justin tried on the size one and a half. They were too small, and Justin couldn't get his foot all the way in. He could fit the size two, but his toe was at the very tip. No room for growth, and who knew when he might get another pair. The size two and a half offered just the right amount of space. He started cheesing.

"How's that?" I asked, already knowing they were perfect.

"These are just right," Justin said and put both shoes on and started strutting around the store. The new Nikes were fifteen dollars more than I'd intended on spending, but I didn't have the heart to tell him he couldn't have them. I had Steve ring them up, and Justin placed his old shoes into the box. Even though I had to listen to him go on and on about how cool his new shoes made him look, the look on his face was priceless.

As we strolled through the mall, Justin spotted a video store that not only sold games, but allowed you to test them out. He didn't hesitate to run inside, and I was right behind him.

"Justin, your mom said we could go to Foot Locker, McDonald's and back home. That's it."

"Aw, Marcus. Come on. Let's just check out a few games. Just for a minute."

"Cool, just for a minute. And then we're out the door," I said.

Once inside, Justin had already picked up a controller and was giving the video game, Madden 2006, a test run.

"Grab a controller, Marcus. I'll show you how to play."

"I already know how to play Madden, dude. I have it at home."

"The new one?"

"Yep, I got it for Christmas."

"Wow. I wish I had the new Madden. Most of my games are old. My mom can't afford a lot of stuff, but I know how to play because my friend got it."

"You be good, and maybe Santa Claus will bring you some new games for Christmas." I had already made a mental note that I was going to save up to buy him the new Madden for Christmas. I knew it was expensive, but if I saved just a little bit over the next couple of months, I could afford it.

"I don't believe in Santa Claus," he said. "That's just some fake fat dude who wears a red suit and talks to little kids at the mall."

"You a trip." I smiled and shook my head.

"Yeah, I know. My mom tells me that." He

laughed. "Now grab a controller so I can whip you right quick."

"You talking a lot of junk, little man. I told you I got this game at home."

"Then you shouldn't be scared. Now quit your yapping and let's see what you got."

He had me wanting to pop him upside his head. But before I could protest, I had a controller in my hand and Justin was whipping me. We were both caught up, and before long there was a Madden tournament going on in the store. Justin had drawn the attention of every customer in the store, and two of the salespersons as they gathered to watch him beat me. For a minute I was embarrassed that a ten-year-old could run rings around me like that, but suddenly it became my sole desire to regain my dignity. I had to beat him at least once. And that's what I spent the next hour trying to do. Completely lost track of time.

"Man, what time is it?" I looked at my arm, and realized I had left my watch at home. "Anybody know what time it is?"

A white guy in a business suit, awaiting his try at beating Justin, looked at his watch. "Six-thirty."

"Aw, man, Justin. We gotta go."

"Just one more game, Marcus, please."

"We can't. I told your mom we wouldn't be gone long," I said, nervously. I didn't know how Beverly would take me keeping Justin out too long. I wanted to be responsible and keep my word to her. "We gotta go."

"Wait, man. I want my try at beating the little guy," Business Suit said.

"Not today, man. We're out of here."

I grabbed the controller from Justin's hand. Set it back in its place. Grabbed his hand and pulled him out of the store. He was complaining the whole time.

As we sat on a bench outside of JC Penney, I pulled my cell phone out of my pocket and called Beverly. She wasn't worried about Justin and actually thanked me for taking him off of her hands for a while. And commended me for being responsible enough to call her. She said that as long as Justin was having a good time and wasn't tired, that we could stay out longer. That relieved my anxiety.

I pulled into the McDonald's drive-through, asked for a cheeseburger Happy Meal and a Quarter Pounder with Cheese value meal. Asked Justin to hold on to the food while I drove us to a small area airport.

"What are we doing here, Marcus?" Justin asked.

"This an airport. We're going to watch the planes take off while we eat," I said. "This is my favorite place to come on a Friday night. Helps me to think."

In the open green field, we found our places right there on the grass. We watched a plane take off and one land, all during the course of our meal. I stole a couple of Justin's fries while he wasn't looking, and he stole a couple of mine, and we laughed about how he had beat me in Madden.

"You should've seen the look on your face, Marcus, when I beat you." He laughed that goofy little laugh of his.

"That's alright," I told him. "I got something for ya."

"What is it?" he asked, still laughing.

"Don't worry about it." I really didn't have anything for him, except for a shattered ego.

It was a hot summer day, but the sun was already starting to set, and there was a light breeze sweeping across our faces. I told Justin to wipe the ketchup from the corner of his mouth, as another plane swooped down for a landing.

After we finished eating, we gathered our trash and then lay on our backs in the middle of the grass. Gazing into the blue sky, we patiently awaited the next plane to either take off, or for one to come in for a landing. It was the most peaceful I'd ever seen Justin, and for the first time that day, he wasn't running his mouth, asking a million questions, or jumping around. He was actually very still, as if he really enjoyed being out there in the open field.

I thought about the times my pop used to take me to the local airport. We'd lie in the grass and gaze into the sky, awaiting the next plane to either land or take off. We would talk about serious things like sex, girls and about the ups and downs of life. Besides fishing with my granddad, times with my father at the airport were my favorite times. We'd watch the sunset together every Friday evening, and talk about things that only Pop and I could share. We'd talk until it was pitch black outside and until the stars arranged themselves in the sky. The crickets would be chirping and the lightning bugs would buzz through the air as if they were enjoying our company. Those were the days.

After Step-Mommy-Dearest came along, times with Pop became few and far between. I was suddenly losing him daily and didn't even know it, until he was gone. We lived in the same house, but rarely had more than a five-minute conversation here and there, when once upon a time we were best friends. I needed him more than ever after the divorce, and he just simply moved on. Before I knew it, he was proposing marriage to someone that he barely even knew. It all happened so fast. Blindsided me. I woke up one morning and not only was my mother gone, but so was my father. I might as well have been an orphan, because that's what I felt like without my parents.

"Here comes another one, Marcus," Justin said softly, as another plane swooped down and onto the small runway. We watched as it descended and its wheels hit the pavement with a loud skid. It was a yellow plane, old and sort of rickety. Its propeller made a tapping noise and the engine skipped a beat every few seconds, as if it was trying to catch its breath. As I glanced over at Justin, and saw how his eyes lit up over something as small as a plane landing, I wondered about his father and where he was. I wondered if he gave Beverly any money or if he just let her take on all of the responsibility of raising Justin. I wondered if he knew that he'd given Justin sickle cell anemia that caused him so much pain in his body. No kid should have to suffer that way.

"Justin, where's your daddy?" I had to know, so I asked.

"He dead," Justin said. "He died when I was a baby."

I suddenly felt sad, realizing that he'd never had a father in his life. No one to take him to baseball games or teach him how to play football or sit on a fishing bank with. No one to teach him about sex and girls and to talk about stuff that boys need to discuss with a father. I felt sorry for him.

"You ready to go?" I asked him.

"Yeah, I'm a little tired," he said, and did look a little fatigued.

I stood and then helped Justin to his feet.

As we drove home, he snored. Snored so loud, I had to turn the radio up. I smiled at my little buddy. I knew

I was too young to be his makeshift father, but I could definitely hang out with his knucklehead a little bit. Show him that I cared. He deserved at least that.

chapter 19

Indigo

The scent of gingerbread and spicy cinnamon always filled our house during Christmastime. The living room was decorated in colorful lights and garland was spread throughout the house. My parents loved to listen to the old Christmas tunes like Nat King Cole's "Christmas Song" and the Temptations' version of "Silent Night." Daddy would try and hit the high notes of every song, as we decorated the Christmas tree and drank hot chocolate together. Putting the Christmas tree up and decorating it with lights and ornaments that I'd made in kindergarten, was a Summer family ritual that Daddy and me shared every single year since I was three years old. Nana was usually there, too, telling us where to place the ornaments on the tree. Mama would be in the kitchen baking her cakes and pies for the holidays. Daddy and I would trek down to the basement, dig through the junk, find the cardboard box with our artificial tree in it, drag it upstairs and we'd get to work. When I was little, he would lift me in the air so I could put the star on top of the tree. But as I got older, I would stand in a chair and put it up there myself. Then we'd sit back and marvel at our work. By the time we were finished, Mama would have something sweet like peach cobbler or sweet potato pie waiting on us in the kitchen. Daddy would tell us funny stories about growing up in Chicago and we'd laugh so hard, and Nana would always catch him in a lie. They always had different versions of how things happened when Daddy was a kid.

This year Nana wasn't here for the tree decorating. But the next morning, Daddy had fired up the pickup truck and headed to Chicago to pick her up. She always spent Christmas with us, and every year I would count down the days until she got there. Then I would count the hours and then minutes until I finally heard Daddy's pickup pull into the driveway. She would always bring me something special in her suitcase, like some diamond earrings or a pearl necklace, or sometimes it was just simply a dozen of her delicious tea cakes, as only Nana could make.

He and Nana were on their way back from Chicago. Last I heard, they were just outside of Chattanooga, Tennessee, which meant Nana would be there in less than two hours. My heart raced with anticipation, and I had already called them four times within the hour, while they were on the road. I'd cleaned my room up twice and helped Mama change the sheets and pillowcases in Nana's room. I had baked a batch of chocolate chip cookies, although Nana wasn't supposed to have sweets—she was a diabetic. But a cookie or two wouldn't hurt her. She could have some sweets, as long as she did it in moderation. Those were her words. She was always trying to justify eating things that she wasn't really supposed to, like ham or bacon that would send her blood pressure to the moon. She had to be watched twenty-four-seven, because she couldn't be trusted. She didn't have much self-control when it came to good food, especially soul food.

I remember one Thanksgiving night when she thought everybody in the house was asleep, I crept downstairs, and busted her with a plate full of chitterlings loaded down with hot sauce.

"What are you doing?" I asked, turning on the kitchen light as she was eating in the dark. The only light flashing was the one in the oven. I don't even know how she was able to see those nasty little pig's intestines in the dark.

"I'm just having a little snack, Indi. Go on back to bed."

"A little snack, Nana? That's a plate full of chitterlings."

"Okay, you busted me." She chuckled. "Can this be our little secret, baby?"

"Nana, you know you ain't supposed to have pork."

I couldn't understand why anyone would want eat chitterlings to begin with, let alone risk their life over them.

"I know, child. I don't need you to remind me. I just couldn't help myself."

"Well, you need to try harder." I suddenly felt like the parent, and she was the child, as I placed my hands on my hips.

"I will. I promise," she said. "Now, can this be our little secret?"

I thought of all the secrets I'd shared with her, made her promise not to tell a soul. She'd always been the best secret-keeper in the world. How could I say no?

"I promise, Nana."

And I'd kept my promise until the next day when she had to be rushed to the emergency room. Her blood pressure had gone through the roof, and I had to spill my guts about what she had eaten. She wasn't mad though. She just vowed never to do it again. And

I made it my duty to make sure of it by watching her like a hawk whenever she visited our house. I couldn't keep my eye on her while she was at her house in Chicago, but I was her designated food monitor whenever she stayed with us. And although she tried, she couldn't get much past me. I knew her better than anyone else in the whole world. And I wasn't going to stand around and watch her kill herself. I wanted her to be around forever, or at least until my grandchildren were a hundred years old. Accomplishing that would take some work.

Before I knew it, I had fallen asleep waiting for Daddy and Nana to get there. I woke up to voices outside my window and rushed over to see who it was. Nana was standing there in her gray winter coat that she'd worn every year for as long as I could remember. Her red knitted hat hugged her head and a red scarf was wrapped around her neck. Daddy was holding on to her old suitcase as she smiled and had a conversation with Marcus. I lifted the window to hear what they were saying.

"So do you know my granddaughter, Marcus? Her name is Indigo."

"Yes, ma'am. We go to school together, me and Indi."

"That's nice." Nana smiled. "Well it was very nice to meet you, Marcus. Why don't you come over for dinner later on? I'm getting ready to go in here and whip up a batch of fried chicken, macaroni and cheese... that's Indi's favorite, some collards. I might even bake a lemon cake."

"That sounds so good, Miss Summer," he said. "I would love to come over."

"Call me Nana. Nana Summer would be just fine, son."

I couldn't believe my ears. Call her Nana? She barely even knew Marcus from a hole in the wall, and here she was telling him to call her Nana. And why was he pushing up on my grandmother like that? I expected my daddy to say something. To step in. To tell Marcus that tonight was not a good night for him to come over. But he just stood there, holding onto Nana's suitcase, not uttering a single word. He patted Marcus on the shoulder.

"We'll see you later son. Why don't you invite your folks over, too?" Daddy said, when he finally did open his mouth.

I was in awe. My daddy never invited anyone over to our house. I could count on both hands the number of times we had guests over for dinner. What was happening to my family?

Besides, I had plans of inviting Quincy over for dinner, or at least asking my parents if it was okay if he came and sat in the living room with me later. I couldn't wait for Nana to meet Quincy. She would love him, and he would love her. They had to love each other. Anything else would be a nightmare situation. But the chances of my parents saying yes to Quincy coming at all, were slim to nothing now.

Marcus Carter was ruining my life.

I slammed the window shut and ran downstairs to meet Nana. Her eyes lit up when she saw me.

"Hey, Nana," I said.

"Well, well, well. If it isn't my favorite granddaughter."

"I'm your only granddaughter, Nana."

"You're still my favorite." She smiled. "You just gonna stand there, or you gon' come over here and give me some sugar."

I literally fell into Nana's arms. I kissed her round cheeks and held onto her for several moments. I missed her more than I could put into words.

"Mama Summer, you made it." My mother gave Nana a hug, as Daddy carried Nana's suitcase upstairs.

"Come here," I said to Nana. "I made you something." I grabbed her hand and ushered her into the kitchen. Led her right to the plate full of chocolate chip cookies that I'd baked. "You can only have two, maybe three."

"Two or three." She frowned. "That won't do me a bit of good."

"We have to watch your sugar, Nana. You know that."

"I can have anything I want. As long as it's in moderation." She laughed. "Now let me try one of those cookies. Just to see if you know how to bake."

Nana sat down at the kitchen table, one of my cookies in her hand. I sat down across from her, ready to catch her up on everything that had gone on in my life since I saw her last.

"Woo, I'm exhausted, Indi." She sighed. "I think I'm gonna go up these stairs to my bedroom and take me a little nap for a bit. I'm gonna get up later and fry some chicken. I invited that young man from next door over. He seems really nice, Indi. You like him?"

"Who, Marcus?" I acted surprised, as if I hadn't eavesdropped on the whole conversation. "He's okay."

"Handsome fella, that Marcus. Have you seen that smile of his? Gorgeous, you hear me? Right gorgeous. If he was a little bit older, or I was a little bit younger..." Nana chuckled and struggled to stand. I rushed over to help her up. "I'm going upstairs for a bit. Rest these old bones for a while."

I remember a time when Nana Summer used to play kickball in the middle of the street with Jade and me. Now she could barely walk a few steps without needing to sit and catch her breath. My poor nana was falling apart right before my eyes, and there wasn't a thing I could do about it.

"How long are you gonna sleep for, Nana?" I asked, not wanting to be selfish, but I'd waited so long just to talk to her. And now all she wanted to do was sleep. How disappointing.

"Just for a little bit, Indi. Why don't you come on up here and lie across the bed with me. You can tell me all about what's his name...Kelsey?"

"Quincy, Nana. His name is Quincy."

"That's right, Quincy."

I followed Nana up the stairs and to her room. Before she could slip her feet from her shoes, I had already done a nosedive and was sprawled across her bed, running my mouth. Telling her about school, and about my new friend Tameka. I told her about the dance team and how I thought I had screwed up my chances of making it, but made it anyway. Before I could tell her about the first time I laid eyes on Quincy, she was snoring, her plump belly moving up and down to its own rhythm. I just wrapped my arms around Nana and fell asleep myself.

Sounds from Daddy's favorite jazz artist, Boney James, shook the walls in our house. The smell of the spices from Nana's fried chicken literally knocked me out of my sleep and onto the floor. Laughter and loud conversations interrupted my thoughts. I slowly opened one eye and the spot where Nana had slept earlier was empty. She'd thrown an afghan over my legs and had turned on a bedside lamp before she left. I stepped into the bathroom and splashed water on my face, and tried to run a comb through my hair before creeping down the stairs to see what was going on.

In the family room, our next-door neighbors joined my parents in a loud conversation about God only knows what. It was as if my father and Marcus's father were in a competition to see who could talk the loudest. There were glasses filled with brown liquor and ice resting on our coffee table. Marcus's father stood, poured himself another drink and said something about the basketball game and how he thought Miami was going to the playoffs.

"You mark my word, Harold." He called Daddy by his first name. He was a taller, much older version of Marcus, but still handsome. He was much thinner than my daddy, who was round like Nana, and more on the short side. Marcus's stepmother was a thin woman, with weave that hung onto her shoulders. Her face was dark, and plain-looking. She wasn't someone who deserved a second look on the street, but she wasn't ugly either. She and Mama seemed to be enjoying whatever it was they were discussing in a side, more quiet conversation. Every now and then they would giggle about something and take a sip from their glasses of wine.

This whole scene reminded me of when Jade's parents would come over for an occasional visit. They didn't come often, just during the holidays and on special occasions. The four of them would sit for hours talking about whatever it was that grown-ups discussed. They would drink and listen to loud music, while Jade and I played together for hours. It was those times that we enjoyed the most, because whatever we asked for we got. When parents are distracted, they let you do pretty much whatever you want. Jade and I would stay outside way past dark, drink all the Kool-Aid and eat all the sweets we wanted without supervision. The parents didn't care, as long as we were out of their hair. Those were the days.

I didn't see Marcus, and only assumed that he was in the kitchen kissing up to my grandmother again. I needed to go in there and give him a piece of my mind. But just as I tried to make a mad dash for the kitchen, Mama spotted me. Stopped me in my tracks.

"There she is," I heard her say to the rest of the adults in the room. "Indi, come here. I want you to meet our new friends."

Sometime during the evening the Carters had graduated from "the neighbors" to "our friends." When did that happen? I slowly walked into the family room.

"This is our daughter, Indigo," Mama announced to them.

"Yes, I've seen her around," Marcus's stepmother said. "Hi, I'm Gloria."

She smiled, and I was glad to know her name so I could stop calling her Marcus's stepmother.

"It's nice to meet you, Mrs. Carter," I said and smiled at Gloria.

"Oh, you can just call me Gloria, baby," she said.

"Okay."

"And this here is Rufus Carter," Daddy announced. "Say hello, Indi."

"Hello," I said softly.

"Indi, you're much prettier than Marcus described you," Rufus said in his baritone, and laughed that deep, strong laugh that had shaken me out of my sleep just a few minutes earlier.

Had Marcus already talked about me to his dad? How embarrassing. Marcus never ceased to amaze me.

I'd seen Mr. Carter millions of times, all laid out underneath his truck, covered in oil and grease from head to toe. I had to admit, he cleaned up well. He reached out his hand and insisted on a handshake. He nearly yanked my arm out of its socket.

"Where's Nana?" I asked.

"I think she's in the kitchen, baby. She and Marcus have been hanging out together," Daddy said. "Go on in there and say hello to him. He's been waiting for you to wake up."

"It was very nice to meet you both," I said to them.

"You, too, Indi," Gloria said. "Don't be a stranger. Come over any time you want to."

"Thank you."

I made my way to the kitchen, where I found Nana and Marcus sitting at the kitchen table, a chessboard between them, and tall mouthwatering glasses of red Kool-Aid sitting there.

"How many of those have you had, Nana?" I asked in my motherly voice, referring to the Kool-Aid.

"This is my first glass, Indi, I swear," she said, taking a drink. "Right Marcus?"

"Right. Her first glass," he mumbled, never taking his eyes off of the chessboard.

"Indi is my sugar monitor and my blood pressure monitor. I have diabetes and high blood pressure, and she makes sure I stay on track," Nana explained to Marcus.

"Oh, I see," he said, and moved one of his chess pieces across the board. "What's up, Indi?" He finally looked up.

"What's up, Marcus?"

"Nana just took all my money, and I'm trying to win it back."

"Y'all are playing for money?" I asked, and that's

when I noticed the stacks of dollar bills next to the chessboard. I couldn't believe they were gambling and on a Sunday, too.

"That'll teach him to mess with an old woman," Nana said.

"You mean, a beautiful older woman." Marcus grinned as he complimented my grandmother.

"Don't be trying to distract me, boy, with your compliments," Nana said and moved one of her chess pieces. "It almost worked, too."

"You are a beautiful woman, Nana," Marcus said. "You and Indi have the same flawless skin. Beautiful black women."

"You hear that, Indi? He thinks we have flawless skin."

"Nana, is dinner ready? Can I eat?" I asked, ignoring the whole exchange between the two of them.

"Waiting for the macaroni and cheese to brown. Then we can all eat together," she said. "Open that oven and see if it's done."

I did as Nana asked. Opened the oven and checked the macaroni and cheese. It had browned nicely.

"I think it's done, Nana." She barely heard because she was so wrapped up with Marcus.

"Take it out, baby," she said. "And go tell the others that dinner is ready."

I placed oven mitts on my hands. Took the casserole dish out of the oven and placed it on top of the stove. Eyeballed Marcus as I made my way into the family room.

"Dinner's ready," I announced. They barely heard me over the music and loud conversations.

I silently wished this night would end soon, but it was just beginning as we sat at the table, said grace and broke bread together.

"How did you all end up on the south side of town anyway?" Daddy asked Mr. Carter at the dinner table.

"Well, you see, Gloria's mother lives over this way. And she's not in the best of health. Gloria wanted to be closer so she could take better care of her."

"That's real nice." Mama smiled at Gloria. "I wish I had spent more time with my mother before she passed. But Mama Summer here has been just like a mother to me."

Mama and Nana shared a smile.

I barely remembered Grandmother Aida. I was four when cancer took her away. Nana had been my only grandmother for as long as I could remember.

"I told Rufus that I wanted to be able to go with Mama to her doctor's appointments and be near just in case something happened. Living in Stone Mountain, we seemed so far away," Gloria said.

"That's when she weaseled me into having us a

house built." Rufus laughed and elbowed my father. "These women can bat their eyes and get pretty much anything they want."

The two of them roared with laughter.

"So you're having a house built?" My mother zeroed in on that comment.

"Well, we were. There was a problem with the builders and the subcontractors, and..." Gloria said.

"And in the meantime, we'd already placed our house on the market, and it sold within two weeks' time," Rufus added.

"We didn't expect it to sell that fast," Gloria said. "So I asked Rufus...I said baby, don't you have a property on that side of town that we could move into temporarily? At least until our house is finished." She took a bite of her fried chicken leg and waved it in the air. After her whole speech about how bad fried foods were, she didn't waste any time loading two pieces onto her plate. "Of course, there was nothing available."

"There never is when you need it," Mama said. "So how did you end up in the house next door?"

"It's the funniest thing. You are gonna crack up," Gloria said, and everyone waited patiently for the rest of the story. Rufus seemed restless at that point.

"Let's talk about something else," he said. "We can't just take over the dinner conversation with our boring story of how we ended up here. The good part is, we moved here, we've met our wonderful neighbors and new friends, and we'll all live happily ever after."

That wasn't enough for me. I wanted to hear the rest of the story of how they ended up in Jade's house, and Gloria was anxious to tell it, so she continued.

"Rufus, I'm telling this story," she said. "Now as I was saying. The woman who used to live next door to you all…"

"Barbara?" Mama said.

"Yes, Barbara," Gloria said. "After her and her husband split up, she had a little trouble paying her rent. I mean this woman was late consistently every single month, and sometimes she didn't even have it all. Always had some excuse for Rufus. So, I told him, baby look, we are trying to run a business here. If she can't afford to live in the property, then she needs to move. We offered to move her into a smaller, more affordable house, but she insisted that she was moving to New Jersey somewhere. And my husband—" she reached for his hand and caressed it "—being the big old softy that he is, has such a soft spot for his tenants. Always bending over backwards to help them, letting them slide on the rent. We can't run a successful business that way, letting people get over on us. He didn't have the heart to kick them out, but

I told him...look, Rufus...you need to ask her to leave or I will..."

"So it's true," I whispered. "Angie was right. You really did kick them out on the street."

"Gloria, I told you it wasn't a good time," Rufus said. "Let me explain...."

"No need to explain, Rufus. Your wife explained it quite well," Mama said. She was just as hurt as I was. Barbara had been her friend, too. In fact Jade's family had been just like family to us all.

"You have ruined my life!" I said. "Jade was my best friend, and you're the reason why she's gone."

Tears trickled down my cheek. I lost control, and before I knew it I was up from the table and running for my room. Someone called my name, I wasn't sure if it was Mama or Nana, but I kept on moving, slamming my door behind me. My heart was aching and I didn't know how to make it stop. All I kept remembering was Gloria's lips saying, "Rufus, you need to ask her to leave, or I will..." I wanted to wrap my fingers around her bony neck and squeeze it until she stopped breathing. I wanted to steal Gloria's life just the way she'd stolen mine.

I knew it was a mistake for Marcus and his mixed-up family to come for dinner in the first place.

chapter 20

Marcus

I would give anything for Indi to understand that I had nothing to do with her friend Jade moving away. I wanted to tell her that I didn't even want to move to College Park in the first place. I was perfectly happy living in Stone Mountain where I had friends at school and a girlfriend who I actually liked. It was all Gloria's idea to move, and Pop had just fallen into another one of her traps. I wanted Indi to know all of that, but she wouldn't open her window no matter how many Skittles I threw. My chances of salvaging our friendship were definitely shot.

Pop had made amends with Indi's parents, and they'd even forgiven Gloria as she'd gone over and apologized profusely. My father and Mr. Summer had watched the basketball game together just two nights ago, and we were even invited over for

Christmas dinner. But Indigo just wasn't as forgiving as her parents. She wouldn't even look my way when I saw her at school, just rolled her eyes and kept on moving. She was hurt. Her best friend had been needlessly taken away and she needed to blame someone. But she didn't understand that I wasn't the one to blame.

"Give her a little time," Nana Summer had said when I saw her resting on the porch one morning before school. "She's a little stubborn."

I did just that. Tried to give Indi a little time. Waited for her to come around, but she never did.

Christmas Eve, and the mall was a madhouse, filled with people trying to finish up their last-minute shopping. I stopped by the jewelry store and picked up the bracelet I had been eyeballing for Sasha. After Indi stopped speaking to me, I latched onto Sasha and held on for dear life. She had filled the void that I had hoped Indigo Summer would fill. Despite the fact that she was Quincy's girl. I knew it was just a matter of time before he played himself, and she would've been mine. But this whole incident with Gloria and Indi's best friend, Jade, had robbed me of my chances forever. Gloria was definitely not on my good list.

I dropped by Sears and picked up Pop a new toolbox, with a bunch of shiny new wrenches and screwdrivers inside. Picked up Gloria a colorful scarf, just so I could say I bought her something. My heart wasn't in it, and no thought had gone into either. But at least I got her something. I grabbed Beverly a wool sweater that I'd spotted on sale at JC Penney's. The saleswoman was nice enough to help me pick it out. That was a gift that I'd put thought into. I had even saved up enough money to get Justin that new Madden he wanted from the video store. I couldn't wait to see the look on his face when he opened that one. And after much searching and although Indi wasn't speaking to me, I had even managed to pick her up the perfect gift. I had planned on giving it to her, even if she slammed the door in my face. Too much effort had gone into it for me not to at least try. Maybe I'd just leave it on the front porch or give it to Nana to make sure she got it.

I'd had Justin's Madden game and Beverly's sweater both wrapped in colorful paper at the mall, tied with a beautiful bow and everything. When I pulled into their driveway, the curtains were drawn and it looked as if they were gone. I didn't have a chance to call before I popped up, but I was sure Beverly wouldn't mind. She loved when I visited Justin. I hopped out of my Jeep and trekked to the front door, rang the bell. No answer. I tapped lightly on the door. Still, no answer.

"They not home." Justin's friend Kevin flew past on his dirt bike.

"You know where they are?" I asked, as he slowed and then popped a wheelie in the middle of the street.

"The ambulance took Justin to the hospital again," he said, and then took off down the block before I had a chance to ask any more questions.

I remembered the route to the hospital and took off toward it at full speed, almost running the stop sign at the end of the block. I wondered if Beverly was alone. She shouldn't have to deal with this all by herself. I said a little prayer as I parked in the visitor's parking area and rushed through the automatic doors. Sasha's face was the first one that I zoomed in on when I searched the waiting area. She rushed over to me. Her face held a look that was foreign, solemn. Something was wrong.

"What's up?"

"He had a stroke, Marcus," she said. She just blurted it out without warning.

"What?" I asked.

"He had a stroke." She repeated it.

"How could he have a stroke? He's only ten years old," I asked. Strokes and heart attacks only happened to old people, I thought.

"I don't know how it happened, but he did. I just happened to be walking past and saw the ambulance lifting Justin into the back. Miss Beverly was all alone and I asked her if she wanted me to ride with her. She said yes." Sasha was talking so fast, I had time to zero out and then zero back into what she was saying.

"Where's Miss Beverly now?" I asked. I had to find her. I needed some answers.

"She's back there," Sasha said. "With Justin. She's probably doing the paperwork or something."

"I have to find her," I said and headed toward the rooms where they stored patients temporarily.

"You can't go back there," Sasha said.

"I need to see Justin. Talk to him."

"You can't talk to him, Marcus," she said.

"Why not?" I stopped and looked her square in the eyes.

"He's dead, Marcus," she said. "He didn't survive the stroke."

It was as if time stood still. I wasn't sure if she said what I thought she did. I was either hearing things or she didn't know what she was talking about. Justin couldn't be dead. I'd just tutored him in math two days ago. My body felt numb. Part of me wanted her to repeat what she said so that I could be sure of it. The other part of me didn't want to hear those words again.

The moment I saw Beverly's face, I knew that Sasha was telling the truth. Her eyes were puffy and red and an older woman was helping her walk. Her legs were like jelly as the older woman helped her to a nearby chair. She cried harder once she sat down, and my heart skipped a few beats as it pounded so rapidly. I could feel the pounding in my throat as I made my way over to Beverly. She glanced up and tried to regain her composure for my sake, but it was useless. She couldn't.

"He's gone, Marcus." She shook her head from side to side. "My baby's gone."

I sat in the chair next to her, fighting the tears with all my might. I wrapped my arms around Beverly and she dropped her head onto my shoulder.

"My baby's gone," she kept blurting out, over and over again.

It was becoming almost impossible to contain my own tears, but I needed to be strong for her. I glanced over at Sasha, who was in tears, too. Everybody was in tears and I was struggling just to keep it together.

chapter 21

Marcus

The walls seemed to be closing in as I lay there staring at the ceiling in my room, the ceiling fan spinning around in slow motion, the ESPN announcer on my television announcing the score from last night's Falcons game. But I was halfway listening because my chest was aching. I could've sworn I was having a heart attack, but then realized I was just grieving. Grieving for a little boy who didn't deserve to die. He was so full of life, and had so much to look forward to. Why would God allow something like this to happen to a child?

I recognized it as grief because it was similar to the feeling I had when my parents divorced, and the pain I felt when my mother took off in the middle of the night. It was even similar to the hurt I experienced when Pop married Gloria. This pain was similar, but so much stronger than any of those things. The way

Beverly cried for her son made me feel helpless. I wished I had words of comfort for her. Wished I could tell her something that would give her hope…something that would change her tears to joy, but I had nothing to offer, except for the stupid look on my face when I said goodbye to her at the hospital. I had no other words for her than that, and that bothered me.

When I told Pop what happened, he and Gloria rushed over to the house to comfort her. Took some food for the family. They asked if I wanted to go, but I didn't feel much like doing anything. Needed to gather my thoughts, regain my composure. That's how I ended up in the center of my full-sized bed, staring at the ceiling fan as its blades spun around and around. At first I was angry. Angry at God for allowing this to happen to Justin. Then I was hurt. Then sad. Then angry again. My emotions seemed to be moving at full speed as if on a roller-coaster ride at Six Flags Over Georgia.

I took a nap, just to see if I could rid my thoughts of Justin and the look on Beverly's face when she discovered her baby was gone, and the way Sasha's eyes were bloodshot when I first saw her in the emergency room. I wanted to rid my thoughts of the Madden video game that still laid on the backseat in my Jeep. The game that Justin would never play. He would never laugh or pop a wheelie on his dirt bike again. That made me angry, and then hurt, then sad and then angry again. A roller coaster of emotions rushing through me, as the walls kept closing in.

It was Christmas Eve, but it felt like D-Day.

chapter 22

Indigo

CHRISTMAS Eve.

My favorite day of the year next to Christmas Day. I always got to open at least one gift on Christmas Eve, and it was like a lottery trying to figure out which package held the best gift. Needless to say, I didn't hit the jackpot, because the one I opened held a pair of socks. My parents were getting to be pretty clever at this gift exchange thing. They had rolled the socks up tightly into a small box so I'd think I was really getting something special, and cracked up at the look of disappointment on my face when I discovered that I'd been had.

"You have to learn to wait, Indi." Mama was the ringleader and her and Daddy laughed.

Daddy even had the camcorder out, getting footage of me opening the box filled with pink-and-white

Nike socks, capturing the look on my face. Even Nana chuckled a little.

"Ha, ha, ha, very funny." I frowned and set the socks aside. "Nana, I thought you were on my side."

"I am on your side, baby. But you have to admit, it *was* funny."

"Can I open another one?" I asked, hoping for another try.

"No," Mama said. "That's against the rules. One gift on Christmas Eve. That's all you get."

"I don't know, Carolyn..." Daddy smiled. "It wouldn't hurt to let her open one more."

"But if we let her open one more, that would go against the tradition."

"Please Mommy," I begged. "Just one more."

"What if you're not happy with that one either?" Mama said. "Then what?"

"Then I'll wait until Christmas morning. I promise."

Nana sat in the corner of the room, a smile on her face, all leaned back in Daddy's recliner, enjoying every moment of the teasing.

"Okay, Indi. One more. But that's it for the night," Mama said.

"Thank you, Mommy," I said, and hugged my mother around the neck.

I made a beeline for the Christmas tree. Picked up a medium-sized box, shook it to see if I could tell what was inside. Observed the faces of the adults in the room, just to see if they would give away what was inside. Their faces were blank. So I slipped that gift back under the tree. I almost went for another small one, remembering that Nana always said that good things come in small packages. But I'd been tricked by a small package that held a pair of socks. So I decided to go for the gusto. Picked up the largest box under the tree that had my name on it. It was huge. And kind of heavy, too. Yes, this was the one. This was the gift of all gifts. It had to be. I didn't waste much time ripping the colorful paper off of the package; tossed it aside. The brown box was plain, no pictures or writing on the outside. I needed something to cut through the tape. This was wrapped pretty good, with the sort of tape that you needed scissors to cut through.

Before I could ask, Mama was handing me a pair of scissors. I looked at her with skeptical eyes as I reached for them. She smiled and winked, as if it was another bogus gift. I didn't care, I wanted to know what was inside, and it wasn't going to open itself. Whether it was a good gift or not, I needed that box opened, and quickly. Suddenly the tape was removed, and the tissue paper was pulled out, piece by piece. I pulled the electronic equipment out of the box, set it on the floor next to me. A stereo! And not just a little boom box like the one I already had, or the portable CD player that I had with the headphones. It was a real stereo; the kind like Daddy had in the family room that he played his jazz CDs on. This was by far, the best gift I'd ever received.

"Can you hook it up, Daddy?" I asked.

"Not tonight, Indi. It's late."

"Please, Daddy? I want to try my CDs out on it."

"Fine," he said. "Let's take it upstairs and see what it sounds like."

By the time Daddy got the stereo hooked up, Christmas Day was only an hour away. I tuned the stereo to *The Quiet Storm* on V-103 and gave in to my heavy eyelids.

At the crack of dawn, loud Christmas music rang through the house. Smells of smoked sausage and onions crept across my nose, and I had to go see what it was. I slid from beneath the covers, tiptoed downstairs. Nana hummed the tune of "Silent Night" as pots and pans rattled in the kitchen.

"Merry Christmas," I said as I peeked my head in.

"Merry Christmas, baby." She laughed. "I should've known you would be up early, before the birds."

"The birds are already up, Nana." I smiled. "I heard them chirping outside my window."

"Cute," she said and touched my nose. "You hungry?"

"A little," I said. "But I'm more curious than hungry."

"Go wake up your mama and daddy," she said. "And then you can terrorize the tree."

She already knew what I had in mind. Christmas gifts first, then food. In that order. I rushed up the stairs and to my parents' room. I heard my daddy's loud snores before I reached the top of the stairs. I slowly pushed the door opened, peeked inside. They were both knocked out. Mama would be the easiest to wake, so I started working on her first.

"Mama," I whispered. "Mother."

Her eyes opened slowly; she was a light sleeper, and smiled at me once she was awake.

"Is it Christmas morning?" she asked.

"Yes, ma'am," I said, and Daddy turned over, making little grunting noises, and then farted.

I frowned and squeezed my nose. Mama didn't flinch. I guess she was used to it, although she did nudge him a bit.

"Harold. It's Christmas morning and our child is ready to open her gifts," Mama said.

He just grunted and readjusted in his sleep.

"Daddy," I called, giving it a shot.

"Harold." Mama nudged Daddy again. This time he opened his eyes at least.

"Good morning, Daddy," I said. "Merry Christmas."

"Who's that child at the door, Carolyn?" he asked teasingly. "Is she lost?"

"It's Christmas morning, Daddy," I said. "We have gifts to open."

"Did she even go to sleep last night?" He eyeballed my mother and asked.

"Yes, I slept last night," I said impatiently. "Now can we go open gifts?"

"We'll meet you downstairs," Daddy said, and gave me a look that said, "now please go away."

I did...go away. Shut their door behind me and went back downstairs to give my parents a chance to wash their faces and brush their teeth. But anxiety had the best of me.

After our ritual gift exchange, I rushed upstairs and showered. Ironed the outfit that I'd picked up at the mall the previous weekend, an outfit that had been carefully chosen with Quincy in mind. I'd tried it on at least six times throughout the week and couldn't wait for him to see me in it. From the moment my feet hit the floor that morning, I started counting down the hours until Quincy would arrive. I'd picked him up a jersey from one of the stores at the Underground, a mall in downtown Atlanta. It was the perfect gift, along with the Burberry for Men cologne that I picked up, too, and had them both specially gift-wrapped. After shopping for Quincy, I barely had enough left to buy those house shoes for Daddy, the sweater from Casual Corners for Mama—they were having a holiday sale—and those sterling silver earrings for Nana. They were small gifts, but hey, I'm a teenager without a job. For Jade and Tameka I would catch the after-Christmas sales. They would understand.

Quincy was supposed to visit with his family for most of Christmas day, but promised that he'd make it to my house by early afternoon. I made him commit to three o'clock. I'd barely talked to him on Christmas Eve or the day before because he had out-of-town guests—cousins, uncles and aunts from Pittsburgh. Things had sort of changed between us since Thanksgiving weekend, our second major date. A date that had landed him at my house at seven, tapping on my front door. We ended up at Steak and Shake for burgers and fries. Afterwards, he announced that he needed to drop by his house for a minute, wanted to make sure he'd locked up because his parents were out of town for the weekend.

"Come on in for a minute," he said, once we pulled into his circular drive.

I followed him inside the huge, two-story house that smelled of fresh paint, and carpet that looked brand-new. It was almost as nice as some of the homes I'd seen on MTV *Cribs,* just not as big. Still carrying my chocolate shake, Quincy showed me around their minimansion. His parents' bedroom looked like a little house all by itself. I dreamed of owning a home like that someday, and having a husband like Quincy to share it with. We'd have two little kids, a boy and a girl, and maybe a Golden Retriever to watch the house while we traveled to the exotic places, like Tahiti, for a vacation.

"What's on your mind?" Quincy asked, after we found ourselves in the downstairs den. I'd plopped down in an oversized chair in the corner of the room. He hit the remote for the television and the surround sound made me feel as if we were at the movie theater.

"Nothing. Just thinking how pretty your house is."

"It's alright."

"Your parents must be rich..." I said "...with a house like this."

"Nah, if they were rich, they wouldn't have to work as hard as they do. This is the first vacation that they have taken in two years," he said.

"I guess you have to work hard if you want nice things, right?"

"That's what they tell me," he said and then grabbed my hand. "Come on. Let me show you my castle."

We trekked upstairs to Quincy's bedroom. It was a huge room, with a tall ceiling. I could put my bedroom inside of his and still have room left over. He had a bathroom right off of his bedroom, with a Jacuzzi tub and separate shower, which he shared with his younger brother, Travis. His room was decorated with a blue-and-green comforter that matched the curtains, and photos of professional football players were carefully organized all over the walls. Some of them were autographed.

"Have a seat." He sat on his bed and invited me to sit next to him.

I knew it was a good time to suggest that we go catch that movie that we were supposed to be catching. That's where I told my parents I would be. But suddenly the plans had changed, and here I was in Quincy's bedroom, while his parents were away, swapping kisses with him on his full-sized bed.

"Just relax," he said as his hands began to touch places on my body that I wasn't even aware existed.

His lips found the back of my neck and he planted kisses there too. Before I knew it, my Chicago Bulls sweatshirt, that Uncle Keith had sent me last winter, was over my head and thrown to the floor. Quincy had removed his shirt and thrown it on the floor, too, revealing his bare chest and a small tattoo on his right arm. I was sitting there in my pink sports bra, chill bumps running up and down my arms, my flesh being seen by another human being, other than Nana or my pediatrician, for the very first time. There were girls who would kill to be in Quincy's bedroom with him, all of their clothes thrown on the floor in a pile next to his. But here I was, desperately trying to come up with an escape plan. A way of saying "no" again, even though it would be the death of our three-and-a-half-month relationship. He was oblivious to the butterflies floating around in my stomach as he continued to leave a trail of kisses all the way down my back.

My cell phone vibrated in the pocket of my jeans. It startled me at first, but then I was grateful for the diversion. I reached for it, and Quincy held onto my hand.

"Let it ring," he whispered and squeezed both my hands.

"I can't," I said. "I have to see who it is. What if it's my parents?"

He shrugged.

I reached for my cell phone again. This time Quincy was patient, as I pulled it out of my pocket and tried to answer it. It was too late. The call was missed, but I pressed a few buttons and found out that it was Jade.

"Who was it?" He asked.

"My father," I lied. "He left a message."

I logged into my voice mail. Entering the password, I listened to Jade's message.

"Hey, big head, it's me. Where are you? You were

supposed to call me the minute you got home from your date with Quincy. Are you still out with him, girl? What did you end up wearing? What did he have on? What did y'all go see at the movies? Did he take you to McDonald's to eat or what? What the heck did y'all talk about? Call me. And hurry up!" She asked a million questions, but only one stuck in my head. "Indi, did you give up the booty? Call me."

"I have to go," I told Quincy.

"What did he say?" he asked.

"He said that I need to get home right away," I lied again. "He sounded mad, too."

"For real?" He asked, rushing to pull his shirt over his head. "Did you do something wrong?"

"Who knows?" I shrugged, and quickly put my sweatshirt back on. "He gets like that sometimes."

Quincy's demeanor changed. He became quiet and standoffish as he ushered me out of his room, down the staircase and through the front door. After that, things were never the same. Even his walking me to class seemed artificial, as if he was just going through the motions. There was no enthusiasm in his voice when we talked on the phone, or when he saw me on Monday after a long weekend. In fact, it was me who did all the calling. If I didn't call Quincy, there was a good chance we might not talk. When he did call, it was in return of my phone call. I sought him out in the mornings before school to say good morning, and rushed over to the football field after dance team practice just to say good-night. Things were definitely different.

Still, I made him promise to come over on Christmas Day.

"I'll try, Indi," he said. "I have relatives from out of town here. It's going to be hard breaking away."

"You have to," I said.

"It will have to be sometime in the afternoon, after I spend time with them," he'd said. "I'll see if I can get my mother's car."

Three o'clock had come and gone. It was a quarter past five and I was becoming restless. I called his cell phone three times, and had left two messages. Christmas was nearing its end, and there was no Quincy. Mistletoe hung in the doorway between the living room and kitchen, a rib roast had been cooked in the oven, cakes and pies were all over the dining room table. Opened Christmas gifts and wrapping was scattered about; I'd received just about everything I'd asked for—a brand-new stereo, gift certificates from Victoria's Secret, Charlotte Russe, 5.7.9, and the Disney store. Every CD I asked for, I got. A leather Gucci purse and a pair of boots were mine too. But no Quincy.

When the doorbell sounded, it echoed through the entire house. I exhaled and shut my eyes for a moment. I didn't want to seem anxious, so I let someone else get it as I observed myself in the bathroom mirror. My eyes were still a little puffy from crying, but they weren't bad. A little Visine would clear them right up. I refreshed my lip gloss and combed my hair.

"Indi," Mama called, and I waited a few minutes before answering. "Indi, you got company."

My heart beat a little faster than its normal pace. I couldn't wait to see Quincy. Even though he was over three hours late, my anger seemed to vanish the moment the doorbell had rung. I walked slowly down the steps and could swear I heard Mel's laughter echo through my house. It was definitely a woman's voice that I heard. It was definitely Mel.

"Hey, Indi," Tameka said. She stood at the bottom of the stairs and handed me a package wrapped in silver paper. "Merry Christmas, girl."

I grabbed the gift, a flood of emotions rushing through my veins. I hoped my disappointment wasn't obvious, as I faked a smile.

"Hello, Indi," Mel said. She was dressed in sexy low-cut jeans and a sexy top. "Santa Claus been good to you?"

"Yes, ma'am," I said, and gave a half smile.

"Open the gift," Tameka urged. "Hurry up."

Inside was a set of silver bangles and a matching pair of hoop earrings.

"Thank you," I said, and hugged Tameka. "These are cute."

"Did Quincy ever show up?" she whispered as we embraced.

"Not yet."

I said "yet" because for some crazy reason, I was still hopeful.

When Mel and Tameka invited me to the movies, I declined.

"Might do you some good to get out of the house, Indi," Nana said.

"Ain't that the truth?" Mel agreed, as the two of them rearranged my evening for me.

"Come on, Indi. Go with us," Tameka said.

I was afraid that if I left my house, Quincy might show up. But after much convincing, I agreed to a movie with Mel and Tameka. Anything was better than sitting at home.

A bag of popcorn in one hand, and a soda in the other, we searched for the auditorium where our movie was showing.

"Here, hold this," I told Tameka. "I have to go

really bad." I bounced around as my bladder was about to explode. Mama told me about holding it until the last minute. She said I would damage my insides by doing that.

I handed Tameka my popcorn and soda and made a beeline for the ladies room. As I swung the door opened, I slammed into a girl coming out. Looked up and discovered it was Patrice Robinson, dressed in a pair of tight jeans that looked as if they were painted onto her body.

"Dang, watch where you going," she said and rolled her eyes when she realized it was me.

"Excuse me," I said with attitude and walked on past her.

"You excused."

After handling my business, I stood in the mirror for a moment. I washed my hands, and made sure my hair was okay. Tameka and Mel waited for me just outside the door. As I strolled toward them, I caught a glimpse of Quincy standing in the line for the concession stand. I dropped my purse at the sight of him. He was dressed in a Michael Vick jersey and a pair of jeans that sagged a little. His arms were wrapped tightly around Patrice's small waist and hers were around his neck, as they gazed into each other's eyes and shared a kiss. Her round hips and overdeveloped body was pressed up against his. He was lost in the moment until his eyes met mine. Instantly he dropped his hand from her waist.

"Hey, Indi, what's up?" he had the nerve to ask.

"Yeah, what is up, Quincy?" I asked.

"You know Patrice, right?" He smiled. Patrice smiled, too, and gave a little superficial wave.

"Hey, Indi," she said.

I didn't even address her. I spoke directly to Quincy. "What are you doing? I been waiting for you all day. You said you were coming by," I said.

"Me and Patrice been hanging out today. She gave me this jersey for Christmas," he said, and turned so that I could see the back. "You like it?"

I just stared at him in disbelief. His mouth was moving, but I had lost track of what he was saying.

"Are you okay, Indi?" Mel asked. Her and Tameka were both by my side now.

"Yes, ma'am."

"He's a loser. You don't need that. Drop him like a bad habit," Mel said, and wasn't whispering.

But I couldn't let it go. "Why are you hanging all over Patrice like that?"

"Me and Marcus is together now," Patrice boasted. "Tell her, Marcus."

"Yeah, tell me Marcus," I said to him.

He didn't say a word. Just stood there looking like the cat who had swallowed the canary.

Suddenly, I felt Tameka's hands on my shoulders.

"Let's go, Indi. Forget him, he ain't about nothing," Tameka said, pulling me away.

"We can leave if you want to, Indi," Mel said. "We can see a movie another time."

I was so happy that she said that, because I was on the verge of tears. Couldn't wait to get outside so I could let them go. I couldn't cry in front of Quincy or Patrice. They weren't even worth my tears.

"You wanna leave?" Mel asked.

"Yes," I whispered, and before I knew it, we were in the parking lot at Mel's car. I didn't even remember how we got there.

My heart was hurting so badly. Worse than anything I had ever experienced. Worse than the whipping I got with Daddy's belt when I cut up at school. Worse than the punishment I received when my grades dropped. So much worse.

My first real boyfriend, and my first real heartbreak all at the same time. It was too much to handle.

chapter 23

Indigo

Christmas Day didn't feel much like Christmas after all.

Mama and Daddy had already retired for the night, but Nana was still up when I got home. She sat in the recliner next to the window, the moonlight hitting her face, reading glasses resting at the tip of her nose, as she flipped through a *Jet* magazine.

"Movie was over that fast?" she asked when I walked through the door. Fighting mad, I snatched my winter coat off, slung it across the chair in the family room. Life was so unfair, and it seemed that God just allowed it to be that way.

"We decided not to go."

"Saw Quincy at the movies, did you?"

"Mel called you?" I asked, and she nodded a yes.

"You okay?" she asked softly, and I'd held onto the

tears up until that moment. They crawled down my light brown cheeks.

"No, but there's nothing I can do about it."

"You wanna talk about it?" she asked. "It always helps to talk things through."

I kneeled at Nana's feet and rested my head in her lap. She stroked my hair, as the tears began to rush down my face like a waterfall.

"No, I don't wanna talk about it," I mumbled, and continued to cry. I had cried all the way home in the backseat of Mel's car, too. "Not right now."

"Okay, then. We won't talk about it right now," she said. "But I do have one thing to say, Indi. You're not the first girl to have her heart broken, and this certainly won't be the last time, either."

"You mean I'll have to feel this way again someday?"

"Most likely, yes." Nana was nonchalant about the whole thing. "It's something that we all go through at some point in our lives."

"You had your heart broken before, Nana?"

"Plenty of times," she said.

"By who?" I asked and sat up. Looked into her eyes.

"I remember when I was a young girl, a little bit older than you are now. There was a young man who lived on the other side of the railroad tracks. His name was Sonny. Sonny Ray. I tell you, I was crazy about that fella. He was handsome, a spiffy dresser, had charisma—he was about eighteen years old at the time. I was probably sixteen, maybe seventeen. Had my head in the clouds for about six months, Sonny did. I mean I was gone, had the biggest crush. Well, one day he decided he was going away. He had joined the United States Navy, and decided he was going to sail the seas. "'Once I get settled, I'm coming back for you, Virginia. That's what he promised. 'I'm sending you a train ticket to wherever I am and we getting married.' I was so excited! Ran around telling everybody, me and Sonny getting married. Just as soon as he get settled, he's gonna send for me."

"Did he send for you, Nana?"

"A whole year went past before I heard from him again. And when he finally breezed through town, he had another woman hanging on his arm, her belly poked out as big as a watermelon. They had gone down to the justice of the peace and got married, and was expecting a child." She leaned back in the recliner. "Needless to say, that was the end of me and Sonny Ray."

"Did you do something? Say something?"

"Wasn't nothing to be said, baby. He had made his choice, and there wasn't a thing I could do about it. My heart was broken for a little while, but I got over it. I survived. It didn't kill me—you see I'm still here. It wasn't the first time and it certainly wasn't the last.

I had many more heartbreaks after that," she said. "You see, baby, we all make choices in this life, and sometimes we hurt others in the process. Sometimes we get hurt ourselves. But as long as we don't die, and we learn something from it, then we have to go on."

"But it hurts so bad, Nana."

"I know it does, baby. But you'll get through it. You're strong, and you're brave. You're a Summer, and you're cut from good cloth." She took my hands in hers, squeezed them and then kissed my forehead. "It's okay to hurt for a little while, as long as you don't stay there. You understand?"

"Yes, ma'am."

"You cry and you get it all out. Don't hold it inside. And when you go back to school after the holidays, you hold your head up high, and you don't drop it for anyone. You walk through those hallways, and you let him see that you've moved on."

"Marcus tried to tell me that Quincy was a dog. But I wouldn't listen."

"Some things we have to discover for ourselves," Nana said.

"I thought Marcus was just saying those things because he wanted me for himself."

"Could be that he wanted you for himself." She was so calm. Nana never got excited about much. She removed her reading glasses and set them and the book on the end table. "Or it could be he just simply cares about you. Didn't want to see you get hurt."

"Well he was right about Quincy, Nana," I told her. "I was so mean to him. Blaming him for Jade moving away. I wouldn't even speak to him when he tried to plead his case. I'm sure he hates me now."

"I wouldn't be so sure about that," Nana said. "Hate is not something you develop overnight. Besides, he came by to see you today."

"He did?" I raised up and looked at Nana in surprise. That cheered me up and made my heart a little lighter. She grabbed my face in her hands.

"He left you something."

"For real? What is it?" I wiped the tears from my eyes with the back of my hand.

"It's over there under the tree." She pointed her head in that direction. "Said he wrapped that one himself."

It was the only gift left under the tree. Wrapped in bright red, silky paper with a big red bow, it looked as if Marcus had wrapped it. I rushed over to the tree, grabbed it and ripped the paper off. Opened the white cardboard box to see what was hidden inside. The red hair was a dead giveaway as I pulled the Raggedy Ann doll out of the box and held it in the air. It was identical to the one I had when I was little, wearing the same cute little outfit. A tear trickled down my cheek. Not only had Marcus remembered what I said about Raggedy Ann, but he had also put some thought and effort into finding the perfect gift for me. He had to have searched high and low for it. They just didn't make dolls like that anymore. That touched my heart. Had me wondering how could he be so thoughtful, when I had been so mean to him.

The tears rushed from my eyes again. A combination of heartache over Quincy and guilt over the way I treated Marcus. I needed to see him, to thank him. To tell him how sorry I was. I slipped my jacket around my arms.

"I'll be right back, Nana," I said. She nodded a knowing nod as I dashed out the door, ran across my yard and ended up on Marcus's front porch. His Jeep was gone, but I wanted to at least ask his father if he knew when he might be home. I rang the bell and waited for response. Killer was inside going crazy, barking as if he'd lost his mind. I rang the bell again. No answer. I stood there for a moment, and then slowly walked off the porch. I rushed back home and stepped inside from the cold.

"He wasn't home," I told Nana.

"Well, he's gotta come home sooner or later," she said, still reading her magazine. "Maybe you can catch him in the morning."

Morning would be too late. I needed to see him tonight, and was willing to wait. Disappointed, I trekked upstairs to my room. Decided to run myself a warm bath, with bubbles floating everywhere. I sat on the toilet with the lid down, braiding my hair as the water flowed in the tub. Once the tub was filled, I stepped in and let the water soothe every muscle in my body. Unfortunately, it wasn't able to soothe my aching heart, so that part of me just continued to ache. According to Nana, this was a process that took some time. Soon I would feel better. I had to believe that.

I decided to wait up for Marcus, and ran to my window every time I heard a car door slam, hoping it was him. But each time, it was someone else. Before long, my eyes became heavy and sleep found me. With Raggedy Ann in my arms, I finally gave in to it.

chapter 24

Marcus

indigo Summer was the most selfish girl I had ever met, and I was done wasting my time on her. She was obviously stuck on Quincy, like some people were stuck on stupid. And to blame me for her best friend moving away, well, that proved just how immature she was. She wasn't ready for a guy like me anyway. It was time I moved on. Sasha was way more mature, much smarter, and better than that—she liked me, respected me. She was there for me when Justin died. She had been just as crazy about Justin as I had been, and she was the only person I could talk to about it. The only person who understood exactly what I was feeling. We made a pact to help each other through it.

Miss Beverly's house was filled with grown-ups, including neighbors, some friends of hers and a few family members. We were all determined not to allow her to spend Christmas alone. There was plenty of food, and people were sitting around talking about grown-folks stuff. Sasha and I slipped out the front door and onto the porch. Although it was a chilly Atlanta night, we pulled our coats tighter and bore the cold. I grabbed her hand in mine. Tried to warm it.

"Sasha, do you think that it was because of Justin that we were brought together—you and me?" I asked. "Like fate or something?"

"I hadn't thought about it that way, but yeah, I guess so," she said. "If it hadn't been for me babysitting him, and you tutoring him, we wouldn't have even met. I'm thankful to him for that, because I like you, Marcus. I like you a lot."

"I like you, too," I said. "And I would really like to take this friendship to the next level."

"At one point, Marcus, I thought that it would be cool if we could be more than friends," she said.

"And now?" I asked.

"I have a boyfriend," she confessed. "He's away in college. He's a freshman at Duke. We've been together for three years now."

"An older dude, huh?" She smiled. "How can you have a long-distance relationship like that?"

"It works for us. There's no pressure. I trust him, and he trusts me."

"What about that kiss the other day? The one between me and you. What was that all about?"

"I don't know. I guess I was just sad because of Justin. There were a lot of emotions rushing through me. I'm sorry if that confused you, Marcus. But I love Drew. My heart belongs to him." She looked at me with those beautiful light brown eyes of hers. "Besides, your heart is somewhere else, too. I don't really know where, but it's definitely not with me. Am I right?"

Honesty flowed so freely between us. That's what I liked about Sasha. She kept it real. I decided to tell the truth.

"There is a girl that I really like. Her name is Indigo Summer. But it doesn't really matter because she has a boyfriend, and won't give me the time of day," I confessed. "The thing is, I know this boyfriend of hers ain't about nothing. He's only after one thing, and that's to get in her pants. And she can't even see it."

"Why don't you tell her that?"

"Been there, done that. She's not interested in hearing what I have to say, so I'm letting her find out for herself."

"I wouldn't be so quick to give up on her. She's going to need you when he finally does break her heart." Sasha was so mature. She was beyond her years in wisdom. "You will be there for her, won't you?"

"I'm not so sure now. She's not even speaking to me, and to tell you the truth, I'm sick of trying."

"My daddy always taught me that anything worth having, is worth waiting for." Sasha smiled. "Is she worth having?"

I shrugged. "I don't know."

"Just as fate brought us together, if it's meant to be with you and Indigo, it will be."

"I guess so," I told her, and intertwined my fingers with hers.

"Can we just continue to be friends, Marcus?" she asked.

"Always and forever," I said, and meant that.

Even though Justin was gone, he was still with us in spirit. He had done a good thing—bringing me and Sasha together.

chapter 25

Indigo

It was almost midnight when Marcus's Jeep pulled up in front of his house. I rushed to my window, peeked through my blinds as he hopped out, wearing a brown leather jacket, a striped shirt underneath, and a pair of jeans that looked brand new. I was willing to bet he got them for Christmas. His hair was freshly cut, and his face clean-shaven.

When his light flashed on in his room, I became anxious. Waited for him to start throwing Skittles at my window, just as he always did when he came home. No matter what time of day or night it was, he always reached out to me. But tonight was different. There were no Skittles against my window. And after a while, his bedroom light went out. It was the first night that he hadn't at least tried reaching out to me. Even when I wasn't speaking to him, he still reached out.

I didn't have any Skittles, but I had some peanut M&M's and threw one at Marcus's window. He didn't respond. So I threw two more, and by the third throw his light came back on. He lifted his blinds and his window and looked at me with a look that I hadn't seen before. One that held no excitement in his eyes.

"What's up, Indi?" he asked dryly.

"Where you been?" I asked. "I been waiting for you all night."

"Waiting for me, why?"

"Meet me at the creek," I said.

"Indi, it's late and I'm tired. Can we just talk tomorrow?"

"It's important," I said. "Meet you there in five minutes."

Before Marcus could protest, I closed my window, and pulled my blinds shut. I slid on a pair of Mudd jeans, pulled a thick sweatshirt over my head, slipped on my sneakers and grabbed my jacket. I tiptoed lightly down the stairs, careful not to wake anyone in the house; didn't want to be questioned about where it was I was going at that hour, especially by Daddy. He wouldn't understand. I slowly pulled the front door opened, crept outside and onto the porch. The cool Atlanta night air immediately brushed across my face, causing me to frown as I braced against it. I pulled my jacket tighter and made my way to the side of the house, and down to the creek behind my house.

When I got to the bottom of the hill, there was no sign of Marcus. Had he stood me up? How could I blame him after the way I'd treated him? I shivered as the cold air reached my backside, had somehow crept up through the legs of my jeans. It was too cold to wait much longer, but I decided to give it a good five minutes before I chalked it up as a loss. I sat on the huge rock, praying that nothing would crawl out of the water or from beneath a rock. Wasn't in the mood for critters tonight.

"What are you doing out here in the middle of the night, girl?" Marcus asked. Startled me, as he walked up from behind.

"Waiting for you." I smiled when I saw him. He was so handsome, even in his plaid pajama pants and hooded sweatshirt. He had on tube socks with the slippers that hugged his feet. A baseball cap was turned backward on his head. "Wanted to tell you thanks for the gift."

"You could've told me that from your bedroom window."

"I know, but I wanted to see you." I flirted with Marcus, my next-door neighbor, who I suddenly found myself attracted to. "Where did you find a doll like that? You had to search high and low for it."

"Can't tell you where I found it. It's a secret."

"I appreciate it. It was very thoughtful. The best gift I got this year."

It was the truth. Although my parents had spent tons of money on the stuff they bought me, I didn't appreciate it as much as I did Raggedy Ann.

"You're welcome," he said. "It's late. Why aren't you in the bed?"

"Because I wanted to talk," I said.

"Talk about what?"

"You were right all along, Marcus. About Quincy. I saw him at the movies tonight. He was with Patrice. She was all up on him and stuff, and he disrespected me right there in front of everybody."

He was unfazed by the news and just looked at me.

"Did you think I was just telling you about Quincy to hurt you?" he asked.

"I thought you were jealous of him."

"I had no reason to be jealous, Indi." He lifted his cap and ran his hand over the waves in his hair. "I told you that stuff because I didn't want to see you get hurt."

"I know that now, Marcus," I told him. "And I know that you didn't have anything to do with Jade moving away either. I'm sorry for that too—for treating you bad."

"Don't worry about it, Indi. I'm not mad anymore," he said, and sat on the rock next to me. "Remember my little friend, Justin?"

"Yeah, the boy you been tutoring in math."

"He had a stroke on the other day, and he didn't survive it."

"You mean he died?"

"Yeah."

"Man, I'm sorry to hear that. I know you were crazy about him," I said, remembering how Marcus's eyes always lit up when he talked about Justin. My heart ached for him. "I hope his mother is okay. I prayed for him once. I guess my prayer didn't get through in time."

"Or maybe it did get through, but God had another plan."

"I don't know. Maybe," I said. "Marcus, are you still interested in taking me to a movie sometime?"

"Nah. It's not really appropriate for me to be taking someone else's girl to the movies," he said.

"I just told you, I'm not Quincy's girl anymore."

"You're not my girl either," he said.

I deserved that, and whatever tongue-lashing he had in store for me.

"That's true." I sighed. It was getting cold, and I was anxious to get inside and to my warm bed. Didn't want to embarrass myself by reaching out to him, and having him reject me. I wasn't prepared for any more hurt. "I'm going inside."

"Cool," he said, and sat there as I stood and headed up the hill. "Hey, Indi."

"Yeah?" I stopped in my tracks. Turned toward Marcus. He was standing now. Waited for him to speak. He started walking towards me.

"You wanna be my girl?" he asked, and in my heart I knew that I did.

I thought back to the time that Quincy asked me that same question, remembered how unsure I was, and even after I said "yes." Remembered thinking, "wow, the most popular guy in school wants to date me." I thought it was a privilege and an honor that he chose me. But after giving it some serious thought, I realized that it was a privilege and an honor for him to have a girl like me. One who was not so quick to give it up to any boy, the first chance she got. I might not be the prettiest girl, or the smartest girl, my body was still a little underdeveloped, and I could still whip all of the neighborhood boys in a game of one-on-one in the middle of Madison Place. Which meant I was a borderline tomboy. But the truth was, I was still made of the good stuff. How did Nana put it? I'm from good cloth.

"Yes," I said to Marcus. "Yes, I will be your girl."

He never said another word, just moved closer to me. Pulled me into his strong embrace, wrapped his arms tightly around my waist, and just held me.

chapter 26

Indigo

Halftime.

My nerves were on edge as I stood in the doorway of the gymnasium, my little short skirt creeping up my backside. My hair flying everywhere as my leotard top hugged my chest. I glanced over at Tameka. She winked, but I could tell that she was just as nervous as I was.

"You ready?" she mouthed.

I nodded a "yes" before the music echoed through the gym. An old school tune, "Brick House" by the Commodores, bounced off the walls as Tameka and I ran to the center of the floor, posted up and began to shake booties. We led the routine for our dance team, shaking to the music for at least three minutes before the rest of the team joined us on the floor for their part. The entire student body cheered as we did our thing. Some people were shaking in the stands. Boys were whistling, and others were clapping.

We performed to three different songs, and after the third performance, sweat poured from my forehead and I used the back of my hand to wipe it away. Miss Martin winked and smiled as we took a bow. I was glad it was over. Glad that everyone remembered their parts, and didn't stumble over clumsy feet. In perfect formation, we exited the gym, shaking our hips as the music trailed off. Quincy was standing next to the bleachers with all of his boys from the football team. Even though football season was over, they still hung together like a posse or something. When I looked up, his eyes met mine. He blew me a kiss, and then wormed over toward me.

"You were good out there, Indi." He smiled. "Girl, you can dance."

"Thanks," I said and kept moving.

"Me and Patrice ain't together no more," he went on to say, and then grinned.

The entire football team heard him and all eyes were on me for a response to his little announcement. I glanced at Tameka, who was pulling up the rear of the dance team line. She shook her head and shrugged her shoulders.

"You wanna go out with me sometime?" Quincy went on to ask. This caught the attention of every person within earshot. It was as if we were on candid camera or something. I stood there, not really contemplating an answer. I already had one. But I was in awe that he would even ask me such a question.

"No, I do not want to go out with you." My hands on my hips. "But thanks for asking."

I took off down the hall and into the girls' locker room to change out of my performance clothes, and into my jeans. Left Quincy behind with his ego on the floor. His smile changed to a frown as his boys talked junk to him. I didn't care. I didn't have any time to waste on Quincy Rawlins. Needed to get changed and back into the gym for the second half of the basketball game.

In the locker room, I pulled my clothes on quickly. Rushed back to the gym, and found my favorite seat on the bleachers behind the team. Marcus was at the free throw line, the ball in his hands as he prepared to shoot. He leaned over, bounced the ball a couple of times and then shot it into the basket. With a swishing noise, it went in. All net. The crowd went crazy. I screamed as he put it in the basket a second time, and the crowd went crazy again. He trotted down court, dressed in his white jersey and shorts. He searched the stands for me and when his eyes finally met mine, I blew him the biggest kiss that I could possibly manage.

After the game I waited for Marcus to get changed.

Our team lost to another school, but Marcus was always in good spirits. Even after a game that we lost. He didn't care about losing, because he wasn't really into sports all that much. He just went out for basketball because he wanted to spend more time with me after school. Dance team practice and basketball practice took place at the same time, and afterwards we hung out. Just about every day.

His gym bag across his shoulder, he headed my way. Planted a kiss on my forehead.

"You okay?" I asked.

"Yeah, I'm cool. It was just a game," he said. "You know sports is not really my thing. I'm just out there for the exercise. And to spend time with you. You know, I still have my Master Plan."

"And just how do I fit into that Master Plan?" I asked.

"I haven't figured that part out yet." He smiled. "But you can rest assured, you do fit somewhere."

"Well, when you figure it out, you let me know."

"I'll do that," he said, and then wrapped his arms around me as we braced for the cold night air.

He held the door for me, as I waved goodbye to Tameka. We didn't hang out as much since Marcus and I started dating. There wasn't much room for her. Besides, she was seeing some boy at another school since she broke up with Jeff. I didn't really know all the details about the breakup, but it had something to do with another girl being pregnant.

I didn't hear much from Jade either. She had found a new best friend at her school in New Jersey, and after awhile, our lives seemed to drift apart. It didn't mean we weren't friends anymore, but it meant that we were changing, growing. Life goes on, even when we don't want it to.

"Come on. I'll race you to the car," Marcus said.

We took off running toward Marcus's Jeep and I left him in the dust. Ended up at the car long before him.

"Why you so slow tonight?" I asked, touching the passenger's door.

"Sore, girl. I been playing basketball all night." He smiled. "Besides, I let you beat me."

"Right. You let me beat you, and the sky is really purple."

His strong arms wrapped around me as I leaned up against his Jeep. His lips touched mine and I shut my eyes and kissed him with passion. Thanked God for Marcus. What I felt for him was hard to put into words. He was more than just a boyfriend. He had become my best friend.

As we drove down I-20 toward the Fulton Industrial Airport, I looked over at Marcus. Smiled. He smiled back.

"You know it's too cold to be out in somebody's field watching planes land and take off," I said.

"It's Friday night. You know that's what we do on Friday night."

"I know," I said. "But it's also the middle of January."

"I'll keep you warm, Indi." He smiled and looked at me with those soft eyes.

"You taking me to Mickey D's afterward?"

"Buying you a Happy Meal," he teased.

"I want a Quarter Pounder with Cheese, dude."

"What you need is a salad with a light dressing on the side," he said.

"You must have me mixed up with Charmaine Jackson." I looked at him cross-eyed, and adjusted his radio station. Tuned it to V-103.

"Oh, yeah, my bad." He laughed. "That was Charmaine who needs a salad."

"You are really silly, Marcus," I said. "I told Nana that boys are stupid."

"Not all boys are stupid. Just some." He smiled that beautiful smile of his as we talked junk to each other.

At that moment, I knew that I loved me some Marcus Carter.